Maria/Stuart

by Jason Grote

A Samuel French Acting Edition

New York Hollywood London Toronto

SAMUELFRENCH.COM

Copyright © 2011 by Jason Grote

ALL RIGHTS RESERVED

Illustration by Carolyn Sewell with permission by
Wooly Mammoth Theatre Company

CAUTION: Professionals and amateurs are hereby warned that *MARIA/ STUART* is subject to a licensing fee. It is fully protected under the copyright laws of the United States of America, the British Commonwealth, including Canada, and all other countries of the Copyright Union. All rights, including professional, amateur, motion picture, recitation, lecturing, public reading, radio broadcasting, television and the rights of translation into foreign languages are strictly reserved. In its present form the play is dedicated to the reading public only.

The amateur and professional live stage performance rights to *MARIA/STUART* are controlled exclusively by Samuel French, Inc., and licensing arrangements and performance licenses must be secured well in advance of presentation. PLEASE NOTE that amateur licensing fees are set upon application in accordance with your producing circumstances. When applying for a licensing quotation and a performance license please give us the number of performances intended, dates of production, your seating capacity and admission fee. Licensing fees are payable one week before the opening performance of the play to Samuel French, Inc., at 45 W. 25th Street, New York, NY 10010.

Licensing fee of the required amount must be paid whether the play is presented for charity or gain and whether or not admission is charged.

Professional/Stock licensing fees quoted upon application to Samuel French, Inc.

For all other rights than those stipulated above, apply to: AO International, 5240 N. Sheridan Road, #814, Chicago, IL 60640; attn: Antje Oegel.

Particular emphasis is laid on the question of amateur or professional readings, permission and terms for which must be secured in writing from Samuel French, Inc.

Copying from this book in whole or in part is strictly forbidden by law, and the right of performance is not transferable.

Whenever the play is produced the following notice must appear on all programs, printing and advertising for the play: "Produced by special arrangement with Samuel French, Inc."

Due authorship credit must be given on all programs, printing and advertising for the play.

ISBN 978-0-573-69941-2   Printed in U.S.A.   #29892

No one shall commit or authorize any act or omission by which the copyright of, or the right to copyright, this play may be impaired.

No one shall make any changes in this play for the purpose of production.

Publication of this play does not imply availability for performance. Both amateurs and professionals considering a production are strongly advised in their own interests to apply to Samuel French, Inc., for written permission before starting rehearsals, advertising, or booking a theatre.

No part of this book may be reproduced, stored in a retrieval system, or transmitted in any form, by any means, now known or yet to be invented, including mechanical, electronic, photocopying, recording, videotaping, or otherwise, without the prior written permission of the publisher.

MUSIC USE NOTE

Licensees are solely responsible for obtaining formal written permission from copyright owners to use copyrighted music in the performance of this play and are strongly cautioned to do so. If no such permission is obtained by the licensee, then the licensee must use only original music that the licensee owns and controls. Licensees are solely responsible and liable for all music clearances and shall indemnify the copyright owners of the play and their licensing agent, Samuel French, Inc., against any costs, expenses, losses and liabilities arising from the use of music by licensees.

IMPORTANT BILLING AND CREDIT REQUIREMENTS

All producers of *MARIA/STUART* must give credit to the Author of the Play in all programs distributed in connection with performances of the Play, and in all instances in which the title of the Play appears for the purposes of advertising, publicizing or otherwise exploiting the Play and/or a production. The name of the Author *must* appear on a separate line on which no other name appears, immediately following the title and *must* appear in size of type not less than fifty percent of the size of the title type.

In addition the following credit *must* be given in all programs and publicity information distributed in association with this piece:

World Premiere: Woolly Mammoth Theatre, 2008

MARIA/STUART had its world premiere at the Woolly Mammoth Theater in Washington, DC in August 2008. The performance was directed by Pam McKinnon. The cast was as follows:

HANNAH	Meghan Grady
AUNT SYLVIA	Naomi Jacobsen
STUART	Eli James
RUTHIE	Sarah Marshall
MARNIE	Amy McWilliams
LIZZIE	Emily Townley

CHARACTERS

STUART
HANNAH
LIZZIE
RUTHIE
MARNIE
AUNT SYLVIA

A note about all of the characters: despite their frequently harsh words, they don't yell. Every one of them, even **STUART**, are shut down, cooking on a very slow boil. If they do explode, they do so only rarely.

SETTING

A unit set consisting of two suburban kitchens. Each side of the playing area is devoted to one of the kitchens. They are mashed together in an incongruous, vaguely Cubist or German-Expressionist way – perhaps the table or counters in Kitchen #1 are contiguous with their differently-colored, -shaped, or -sized equivalents in Kitchen #2.

Both kitchens possess an oppressive, suburban, synthetic quaintness. Kitchen #1 is in a 90s-era McMansion in Bucks County, PA. It is all eggshell sheetrock walls and beige plasticine fake wood, and is drenched with the warm, blinding glint of an unobstructed autumn sun. Clutter lies around the place, mostly unopened mail and kitchen paraphernalia. Kitchen #2 belongs to an older house in Bergen County, NJ, 50s/60s era, smaller but probably more expensive. It is shadier and features a blue-violet color scheme that is, in its way, just as oppressive as Kitchen #1's beige. It is less cluttered than Kitchen #1, but no homier – it is overdetermined with stenciling, lace, and small cute items.

Music: contemporary, haunting, pretty, ominous, sexy.

Special thanks to:

Brooke O'Harra, Pam MacKinnon, Howard Shalwitz, Miriam Weisfeld, and the Spiegel family. Thanks and apologies to Friedrich Schiller.

1. Infinite Secret Treasures Rise From Nowhere

(Kitchen #1. **STUART** *draws pictures of superheroes in a large sketchpad while he talks on a cell phone. In addition to the usual clutter, there are boxes, some opened, containing crumpled newspaper and what appear to be old childhood items of his.)*

STUART. So like I was saying, he fights Lukov, right, there's this whole Uh topical, like these Russian gangster capitalists, right, no, it

Yeah, that's his n – American Male, right

That's because the rights were, no one was publishing him since like 1947, except for –

Yeah I know it's a stupid name, I think it had something to do with, he was a mailman in his Uh secret identity

He's like Captain America, sort of, people think he's a knockoff but actually, in actuality, he was created first, like a year or so before, eight months to be exact, but anyway Yeah everybody's really excited Dipal's totally shopping the film rights around

Very funny, no, like a real, legitimate movie, I know it sounds like gay porn, it was a more innocent time.

We can't change it, it's this whole branding thing, if we don't capitalize on the But do you want to hear about this or not?

Hannah?

OK OK so American Male goes to like Azerbaijan, tracking this whole, like Uh terrorist network, and eventually the clues lead him to St. Petersburg, and he's in the Winter Palace, it's going to be great, I got all these reference photos off the Uh internet, right? And then this Russian super-team confronts him, now these guys are mine, Ward Number 6, they're called, they're like these Soviet-era Cold War super-heroes, but we don't know who exactly they're working for now, right, and they're made of, the first member is Ivanov, he's like this pre-Christian Pagan God, then there's the Three Sisters, who are like these three eerie ageless Russian girls who communicate telepathically and when they all hold hands something blows up or something, I'm still working on that one, and The Seagull, who is, you know, like a guy with wings, and he has this helmet that sort of looks like a seagull's head, and then there's the Cherry Orchard, who has all the powers and abilities of, you know, a cherry orchard, I mean its like American Male looks up and he's caught in a cherry tree, or like there's this whole maze, of this like cherry orchard, and Ward Number 6 is chasing him through it, but it keeps changing shape on him, and then finally there's Uncle Vanya, who is their leader, who is this jolly fat guy who's ex-KGB and doesn't have any superpowers.

So what do you think?

I don't know yet, I think maybe they'll just fight but then team up or something.

Yeah, no, I had to invent some new villains, the only one he had when Dipal bought him was this one Nazi guy, though actually he had two enemies but one of them was like this totally offensive Japanese stereotype, like buck teeth, slanted eyes and like bright yellow skin, so anyway he's out. Though we're thinking of making him this like Yakuza guy, or maybe an Asian-American computer whiz who does like martial arts which I realize is also kind of stereotypical, but we'll make him really good-looking. Besides Dipal's Asian and he's I mean he was born in India but

So anyway what do you think?

The characters? Ward Number 6?

They're all, the character names all come from Chekhov plays.

Anton Chekhov?

STUART. *(cont.)* A writer. From Russia? Wrote short stories, plays, Ward Number 6 was a

No I'm

Well that's

I'm thinking about it but

Well yeah but

OK but

A lot of people know who he is

OK OK OK OK OK

How's uh.

That's great. Are you. Yeah.

No that's great yeah. I would love to see the Uh

I love those chrome uh whatchacallits

She's fine. The same.

*(**HANNAH** appears before **STUART**. Except she's not **HANNAH**; she is a **SHAPESHIFTER**. **STUART** does not know this. **HANNAH** is alarmingly beautiful, like an exotic sea creature. She wears a smock with large pockets in the front. The pockets are filled with talcum powder.)*

What…What are you. When did you get here?

(beat)

(overlapping at the *)

You're standing right here. No, how did you, you're standing right here in front of me. But.

Where's your. Phone? No wait, this is like. You're not in Dumont, you're Uh I swear to god you're* right here –

SHAPESHIFTER/HANNAH. *(overlapping at the *)* Hep hep hep hep!

STUART. Uh

*(The **SHAPESHIFTER** marches to a fridge [may be indicated or offstage]. She grabs a two-liter bottle of soda and chugs it, perhaps making a mess of herself.)*

Uh I uh

*(She offers some to **STUART**.)*

STUART. *(cont.)* No I'm still here but.
No thank you I have a juice
I'm talking to her. You. Her.
(overlapping at the *)
*Do you speak German? Because I think that's uh. Can you hear that? Listen! OK OK I'll call you back but you can hear that right?
Right?
(hangs up, stares at her for the rest of it)

SHAPESHIFTER/HANNAH. *(with enthusiasm; overlapping at the *)*
*Freunde, nicht dieser Töne!
Sondern lasst uns angenehmere
anstimmen, und freudenvollere!
Freude, Schöner Götterfunken,
Tochter aus Elysium,
Wir betreten feuer-trunken,
Himmlische, dein Heiligtum!
Deine Zauber binden wieder,
Was die Mode streng geteilt;
Alle Menschen werden Brüder,
Wo dein sanfter Flügel weilt.
Wem der grosse Wurf gelungen,
Eines Freundes Freund zu sein,
Wer ein holdes Weib errungen,
Mische seinen Jubel ein!
Ja, wer auch nur eine Seele
Sein nennt auf dem Erdenrund!
Und wer's nie gekonnt, der stehle
Weinend sich aus diesem Bund!
Freude trinken alle Wesen
An den Brüsten der Natur;
Alle Guten, alle Bösen
Folgen ihrer Rosenspur.
Küsse gab sie uns und Reben,
Einen Freund, geprüft im Tod;

Wollust ward dem Wurm gegeben,
Und der Cherub steht vor Gott.
Seid umschlungen, Millionen!

SHAPESHIFTER/HANNAH. *(cont.)* Diesen Kuss der ganzen Welt!
Brüder über'm Sternenzelt
Muss ein lieber Vater wohnen.
Ihr stürzt nieder, Millionen?
Ahnest du den Schöpfer, Welt?
Such'ihn über'm Sternenzelt!
Über Sternen muss er wohnen.

(At the conclusion of the poem, the **SHAPESHIFTER** *abruptly starts rifling through cabinets, looking at plates and glassware quizzically, sniffing them, trying to take a bite out of some of them, casually tossing them on the floor upon discovering that they are not what she is looking for. Some stuff might break, but it doesn't necessarily have to – she is not being particularly aggressive, just careless.)*

(She takes her time. She appears to be looking for something very specific.)

STUART. Hannah. What are you doing. What are you doing, stop, stop it, my mom's gonna kill me, knock it off
I mean are you.
Can I help you find something?

(re: a glass she holds)

Hey not the Flintstones glass, come on, that's like a. On eBay that's like.

(He saves the glass from her.)

(She raises her heads, sniffs; she smells something.)

(She tears open one of **STUART***'s boxes and rifles through it.)*

Come on, stop.

(She takes out a bust of Friedrich Schiller, wrapped in old newspapers. It has seen better days, and may or may not

be recognizable as the German Romantic writer. Perhaps it has been broken and glued back together a few times, or attempts have been made to paint it funny colors.)

What are you doing to Schiller? No, come on, don't.

(She smashes the bust. She takes an old pink envelope, containing a thick and often-read letter, from inside the bust. She sniffs it deeply.)

SHAPESHIFTER/HANNAH. Look. It is French.

STUART. What are you doing. Will you please give that back please.

SHAPESHIFTER/HANNAH. This closet holds the secret of my lady.

STUART. What

SHAPESHIFTER/HANNAH. Es ist Zeit.

(beat)

It is time.

STUART. Time for what.

Hannah?

*(The **SHAPESHIFTER** takes large handfuls of talcum powder from the pockets of her smock and blows it at him, creating a huge cloud.)*

SHAPESHIFTER/HANNAH. Poof.

(And with that, she leaves.)

STUART. Uh

(Out on him.)

2. Everything Royal Has Been Taken From You

*(Kitchen #2. **LIZZIE** chops vegetables. **RUTHIE** sits at the table. Perhaps **RUTHIE**'s walker stands next to her. Every so often, **RUTHIE** picks grapes off of a fruit platter but does not eat them.)*

*(Silence. **RUTHIE** considers a grape.)*

RUTHIE. Even Werther agrees about the sizes. Of the portions.

(pause)

He says they're too big, everyone says they're too big. The roast beef was good though. Except there were lumps in the gravy. And they had mashed potatoes, and stringbeans, but so much! The mashed potatoes I mean, not the stringbeans. I like the stringbeans with just a little bit of margarine on them, I mean I have to have some pleasures in life.

(pause)

Also they have a salad bar, with lettuce, and tomatoes, and cucumbers, and croutons, and on the other side seven different kinds of dressing, and potato salad, and macaroni salad, and waldorf salad, have you ever had waldorf salad?

(pause)

Have you ever had waldorf salad?

LIZZIE. *(coldly)* No.

RUTHIE. Oh it's the best! They put celery in it, and green and red apple, and little miniature marshmallows, and raisins, and walnut, and they put the whole thing in some mayonnaise, and oh! It's divine.

(pause)

I can eat that all day.

(pause)

RUTHIE. *(cont.)* Werther likes it too but not as much as me. I always complain to the black ladies at the dining room that the portions are too large but then I go up to the salad bar and take two or three scoops of waldorf salad! Werther always says:

(bad German accent)

"You are always eating so much waldorf salad that you are going to turn into a waldorf salad!"

(pause)

He's so funny, Werther. When we went to Atlantic City, that's when I could take the bus, he would say, "The first thing I am going to do is take in the dancing girls!" And I would say, "What about your wife?" And he would say, "My wife, she can't even remember who I am, why would she care if I was looking at some dancing girls! She can't remember anything!"

(laughs)

She has Alzheimer's!

(RUTHIE *laughs at this story, a bit too gleefully. Beat.)*

LIZZIE. Why do you keep picking grapes off and not eating them?

RUTHIE. What?

LIZZIE. You keep picking the grapes off the fucking thing and just rolling them around in your hands and not eating them.

RUTHIE. That's my bad ear I can't hear you

LIZZIE. I don't care if you eat them all, they're only fucking grapes, we can afford plenty of grapes but if you don't want to eat them why do you keep picking them off?

RUTHIE. That's my bad ear you know that

(Overdramatically, like a petulant teenager, **LIZZIE** *stops chopping vegetables and marches to* **RUTHIE***'s good ear.)*

LIZZIE. WHY ARE YOU PICKING THE GRAPES OFF IF YOU DON'T PLAN ON EATING ANY OF THEM?

RUTHIE. You don't have to yell.

LIZZIE. *(overlapping at the *)* Why do you keep *picking the grapes –

RUTHIE. *(overlapping at the *)* *My dentures
The skins get stuck in there and it irritates me

LIZZIE. OK fine then why do you keep picking them off the thing?

RUTHIE. It feels cool, the grapes are cool. It feels nice in my hands.

LIZZIE. You're the one who keeps making me turn the heat up.

RUTHIE. I'm sorry I don't mean to be so much trouble, you can just take me back to Riverdale if I'm too much trouble.

(Overdramatically, LIZZIE marches across the room and goes back to chopping vegetables.)

LIZZIE. *(calling off)* HANNAH!
Where is she it's like she's a fucking teenager

RUTHIE. What?

(Silence. LIZZIE chops vegetables.)

LIZZIE. Oh Jesus Fuck.

RUTHIE. What? Did you cut yourself?

LIZZIE. *(says "Hamburg" like "Ham")* That son of a bitch is off to Hamburg for a week and a half, no help at all with this dinner that bastard and what kind of olives does he get me? I very explicitly gave hom a shopping list, the one fucking thing I asked him to do and now what am I supposed to do with these? My instructions were very explicit, Kalamata olives, and what is this shit?

(She throws the container of olives, hard, sending them flying everywhere, and sobs over the counter.)

(pause)

RUTHIE. Your father always made me get olives, that was the one thing he always made me spend money on, I wanted to buy the Shop-Rite ones because why spend the extra money? But your father always insisted on his special kind of olives. And the worst of it was he wouldn't even eat the actual olives! He would just pick out all of the little red pimentos one by one until he had a whole little pile of pimentos, and that was back when he smoked so just forget it, and he would eat the pimentos with a fork, and I would have to throw those fancy expensive olives out because I wasn't about to eat them.

*(Still crying, **LIZZIE** marches over to where the bottom of a staircase might be.)*

LIZZIE. HANNAH WILL YOU GET THE FUCK DOWN HERE

RUTHIE. You don't have to yell so loud! Is she deaf too? If she's not she will be soon.

*(Silence. **LIZZIE** cries, chops.)*

*(**HANNAH** enters. She is the same person we saw earlier, but no longer strange. There is no trace of the **SHAPESHIFTER** in her appearance or behavior.)*

HANNAH. What?

(noticing the olives)

Jesus.

LIZZIE. Where have you been?

HANNAH. Why is there olives all over the place? Hi grandma.

LIZZIE. Where were you?

HANNAH. On the phone with Stuart.

LIZZIE. How is he. Is he coming?

HANNAH. He sounds slightly crazier than usual. And yeah he said he's coming.

RUTHIE. Did you say you were talking to Stuart?

LIZZIE. I need you to do me a favor.

RUTHIE. How is he?

HANNAH. He's fine.

LIZZIE. Your fucking father neglected to do the one thing I asked him to do which was buy the items on the list I gave him and I need you to go to the store and pick up some Kalamata olives.

HANNAH. How I don't have a license anymore

RUTHIE. I always used to say to Stuart that he was my favorite grandchild but not to tell you so you wouldn't get jealous.

HANNAH. ...

That's great grandma.

LIZZIE. *(overlapping at the *)* What do you mean you don't have a license? I paid all that *money for driving school –

HANNAH. *(overlapping at the *)* *Dad paid for driving school, that was ten years ago and you're still talking about it, anyway I just don't have one, it expired, I was drunk one night and I forgot my billfold in a bar or a cab or something, it was a Jersey license, you know what a nightmare the DMV is, I'm sorry.

(LIZZIE cries again.)

Oh for god's sake.

Listen I think I'm going to stay in a hotel from now on when I visit.

(pause)

RUTHIE. I think she's just upset about the olives.

HANNAH. I'm sorry, but how am I supposed to sleep on that thing? It's like a storage room in there anyway! The room has become like a graveyard for gifts you don't want but can't bring yourself to throw away.

LIZZIE. *(indicating RUTHIE)* Sh!

RUTHIE. What?

HANNAH. Oh she doesn't care and you don't either.

LIZZIE. Fine, OK, if I go to the store to get the olives can you please chop these vegetables for me? And not fuck it up?

RUTHIE. *(maybe leafing through a news magazine)* Bill Clinton, he seemed nice, but then he did all that stuff. Now there's George Bush, who is apparently not the other one but his son, and I never liked him so much, but Werther likes him. But you know who they have now? Hillary! I knew it!

HANNAH. *(to LIZZIE)* Yeah fine.

LIZZIE. Thank you.

(LIZZIE storms out. HANNAH chops.)

RUTHIE. Hannah you're so pretty.

Do you have a job yet?

HANNAH. I have the same job I had last year and the year before that.

RUTHIE. A real job I mean.

(pause)

RUTHIE. Is Rocky coming by?

HANNAH. Rocco. I don't know I have to call him.

(pause)

RUTHIE. Did you hear about the Weissman's girl, Paulette Weissman?

HANNAH. I don't know them, Grandma.

RUTHIE. She went to high school with your mother I think. She lost her hands, she doesn't have any hands anymore. They said she tried to kill herself by lying down on the railroad tracks but she must have changed her mind at the last minute because it just ran over her hands. The conductor said he saw her but it was too late to stop.

She said it dragged her for almost a mile. The wheels on the train, they were hot, it what do you call it, it cauterized the, um, the stumps. It saved her life but the train dragged her for a mile and her mother told me that all she wanted to do was sleep but every time she closed her eyes that was all she could see, was getting dragged by the train.

Tsk.

(pause)

HANNAH. *(sad)* ...That happened a long time ago grandma.

RUTHIE. Oh yeah?

HANNAH. Yeah. That was Aunt Sylvia.
In like the 70s.
Do you really not remember?

RUTHIE. I never forgave him for it.
That's why I burned them, you know. The what do you call them.

HANNAH. Burned what? What are you talking about, Grandma?

RUTHIE. Oh I don't know.

(silence)

SHAPESHIFTER. *(O.S.)* Hep hep hep hep!

RUTHIE. What?

HANNAH. I didn't say anything.

(Silence. **HANNAH** *chops. Out on them.)*

3. His Rudeness Is His Usefulness

(Kitchen #1, an hour or so after we last saw it. Things are still a shambles from the Shapeshifter's rampage.)

(STUART sits at the kitchen table, trying to repair the Schiller bust with Gorilla Glue, making an even worse mess of things.)

(MARNIE enters. She halts, stares at the mess, and STUART, in disbelief and the beginnings of rage.)

(She blinks, takes a deep breath, exits.)

(STUART either does not notice or he has been avoiding her. He works on Schiller.)

(MARNIE enters again. She stares at STUART, and the mess. She's pissed off to the point of shock.)

STUART. *(startled)* Oh hey Mom

MARNIE. What happened to the kitchen

STUART. Uh.

It was uh kind of uh weird.

Actually.

I'm going to clean it up, I just had to

Schiller broke.

There was a, uh. Forget it. I'm sorry, I'll clean it up, I.

(MARNIE looks as if she might cry.)

Aw Mom don't

I'll clean it up, I.

MARNIE. I have to pick up your Aunt Sylvia from the home. Lizzie deals with Grandma and I deal with Sylvia.

I have to pick her up from the halfway house in Long Branch before we can go to Lizzie's.

STUART. I know, I'm coming with you.

MARNIE. I need you to be on my side today. OK? I really really need that. I really need you to be on my side.

STUART. I am on your. Side.

MARNIE. ...

You got gorilla glue all over the table.

STUART. Yeah I uh. What time are we going?

(She storms off.)

STUART. Mom?

When are we leaving?

I mean I can get all this cleaned up.

Before we.

Uh.

(But she is long gone. He looks around at the mess. He starts to clean.)

(blackout)

4. Your Speech Of Comfort Is My Death Sentence

(Kitchen #2, later. The olives from **LIZZIE**'s *outburst have been cleaned up.)*

*(***HANNAH** *has finished chopping the crudite and sits, munching carrot sticks, as* **RUTHIE** *continues to fondle individual grapes.)*

(An awkward silence, one that has probably been going on for a while.)

RUTHIE. You probably shouldn't eat all of those.

HANNAH. All of what. The carrots?

RUTHIE. You'll turn orange. From the vitamin A.

HANNAH. I'll be OK.

RUTHIE. Well your mother will get angry if she gets home and there are no carrot sticks left.

HANNAH. She'll get over it.

RUTHIE. *(conspiratorially)* I think she's very anxious about this party.

HANNAH. I can just cut some more carrots grandma.

RUTHIE. What?

(no answer)

What? That's my bad ear.

HANNAH. Nothing.

(pause)

RUTHIE. I talked to Helen.

(no answer)

I talked to Helen.

HANNAH. Who's Helen?

RUTHIE. Helen who used to live next door to me when I lived at Sylvan Glade. Remember? She used to always give you unsalted peanuts.

HANNAH. Oh yeah.

How is she?

RUTHIE. Oh, I never liked her. She was always so dour.

She got a little dog. I don't know where she finds the energy to take care of it.

And she got a computer, her son set it up for her, he brought it home from the store and set it all up. She told me I should get a computer too and we could chat on it, and I said, "We're chatting right now!"

(*pause*)

I suppose if we did that we could save money on the phone bill and also I wouldn't have to listen to that dog yapping.

But I can't type because of my arthritis and anyhow it's all too complicated for me.

HANNAH. Well tell her I said hi.

RUTHIE. Oh, we don't talk. She'll probably be dead the next time I see her.

(*pause*)

HANNAH. You want a carrot?

RUTHIE. Oh I can't eat those.

You should put some dip on it, that French Onion Soup Dip with the sour cream is so good, I don't see how you could just eat the carrots and celery sticks plain without any of the dip on it.

HANNAH. I'm good like this, Grandma.

(*pause*)

RUTHIE. So pretty.

HANNAH. Thanks.

(*pause*)

(*a pall*)

(**HANNAH**'s *phone rings. She looks at the caller ID, answers.*)

HANNAH. *(cont.)* What's up.
   No I'm in Jersey.
   OK.
   Well could you come get me?
   That's not what you.
   Yeah but that's not what you.
   OK you don't understand, I'm stuck here.

   (stage whisper)
   I'm stuck here with my grandmother
   No my mom's at the store…

RUTHIE. Is that your mother?

HANNAH. No it's Rocco
   No I was talking to my.
   Jesus Christ Rocco, you told me you were.
   OK, no, fuck that

   (to RUTHIE)
   Excuse me, Grandma.

   (HANNAH goes out onto the deck to argue with Rocco. If we can see outside through a window, we can see that she is having a very impassioned phone argument.)

RUTHIE. …

   (She stares, fondles grapes. She is frightened of the silence.)

   (She hums. This can be tuneless and mumbly and continue for as long as seems right.)

   (ad lib as needed) Hmm hm

   (She cranes around to look for HANNAH. If we can see HANNAH, she is still arguing.)

   (Sound of wind rises, maybe some distant thunder.)

   (calling off) You shouldn't be out there in this!
   Hannah?
   You shouldn't be out there in weather like this talking on the telephone!
   Hannah!

*(The wind kicks up, perhaps agitating shutters or a screen door. If we can see **HANNAH**, she huddles for protection.)*

(Sound of a door opening, off.)

*(**LIZZIE** enters. She looks weird. This is because she is not **LIZZIE**, but the **SHAPESHIFTER**.)*

*(She stares at **RUTHIE**.)*

RUTHIE. *(cont.)* Did you get your special olives?
Where's your bags?
Hannah's out on the deck talking on the phone. I told her not to eat so many carrots but she didn't listen.
Where's your bags?
Lizzie?

SHAPESHIFTER/LIZZIE. Hep hep hep hep hep!

RUTHIE. …

SHAPESHIFTER/LIZZIE. Arroganz fand von Unschuld statt,
Sie ehrten und zeigten Ihre Schande mit Stolz an.
Ach, ließ ewige Ruhe
Schlucken Sie diese Tat.

RUTHIE. Lizzie?
…Honey?

*(The **SHAPESHIFTER** takes a warm bottle of soda from the counter. She opens it, ignoring any foam that issues from the bottle, and chugs it, making something of a mess.)*

(as she does this) What are you doing, that's not even cold, you're making a mess of yourself, STOP IT!

SHAPESHIFTER/LIZZIE. But you, I know you, and you are not fallen.
I love you as I love myself.
There are spirits who dwell in unguarded minds, commit all kinds of vileness, and return to hell, at which the stained heart wakes,
Aghast.

(The **SHAPESHIFTER** *slowly and deliberately moves to* **RUTHIE** *and kisses her slowly on the mouth, her face sweet and sticky with soda.)*

*(***RUTHIE** *acquiesces for a split second and pushes her away.)*

RUTHIE. What are you STOP THAT

(The **SHAPESHIFTER** *backs away, then presents* **RUTHIE** *with the pink letter that she took from the Schiller bust.)*

(beat)

*(***RUTHIE** *takes it, reluctant.)*

(Something happens.)

SHAPESHIFTER/LIZZIE. Poof.

(The **SHAPESHIFTER** *exits, weirdly.)*

(beat)

*(***RUTHIE** *looks around, scared. Terrified, in fact.)*

*(***HANNAH** *does not enter. If we can see her, she is oblivious to all of this.)*

*(***RUTHIE** *worries the pink envelope. She smells it. Something familiar.)*

(Wind kicks up outside.)

(She takes the letter out of the envelope and reads it. She might have some trouble with this.)

(She makes out what the letter says.)

Oh.

Oh, no.

(She looks around her. She spots a wastebasket across the room.)

(With great effort, she pulls herself to her walker and begins an arduous journey across the room to the wastebasket.)

(…)

(After a while,)

(…)

(She gets to the wastebasket, but she can't figure out how to get it open. She tries anyway. She has to toss this thing.)

(In attempting this, she slips.)

(But is caught by **HANNAH**.*)*

HANNAH. Jesus, Grandma!

What are you doing?

RUTHIE. Nothing.

I had to throw something away.

HANNAH. You should have just left it. I can throw it away for you.

RUTHIE. *(hiding the letter in a sort of obvious way)* No.

HANNAH. What is that? Why are you hiding it?

RUTHIE. It's nothing, I'll take care of it later.

HANNAH. OK whatever.

(notices the soda mess)

What the hell happened here?

RUTHIE. It was. Your mother. I don't know what she was. Doing.

HANNAH. She came home?

*(calling after "***LIZZIE***")*

Mom?

RUTHIE. She left again, it was very strange

HANNAH. *(calling off)* Mom?

(to **RUTHIE***)*

Come on, let's get you. Sit down.

(calling off)

Mom?

Mom?

RUTHIE. Don't leave me alone again.

HANNAH. I'll be right Um. Hold on.

(She goes off, looking for **LIZZIE**.*)*

*(***RUTHIE** *frantically looks for a place to hide the letter. She puts it in her purse, reconsiders, then puts it under a placemat, or somewhere equally obvious.)*

*(***HANNAH** *returns.)*

HANNAH. *(cont.)* Did she forget something or something?

RUTHIE. I don't know.

HANNAH. Something smells like…something. It's like. When I was a…

Do you smell that?

RUTHIE. *(lying)* No I don't smell anything.

HANNAH. …

You OK?

RUTHIE. Fine.

HANNAH. Whatever.

(Sound of the door, off. They freeze.)

*(***LIZZIE** *enters, with a shopping bag.)*

LIZZIE. Three places to get the goddamn Kalamata olives. It's not like they're rare. It's like there was a run on Kalamata olives or something What the fuck happened here?

*(***HANNAH** *looks to* **RUTHIE**, *who looks on the verge of tears.)*

(beat)

HANNAH. It was me. I went to get a soda, it spilled. I was about to clean it up.

LIZZIE. Well see that you do? Because the last thing I need is everyone's shoes sticking to the floor, like

(demonstrates)

HANNAH. I'm cleaning it.

*(***HANNAH** *cleans.* **LIZZIE** *resumes preparing food, perhaps munching on olives.)*

*(***RUTHIE** *looks terrified.)*

(**LIZZIE** *notices the letter. It is familiar.*)

LIZZIE. What's that?

RUTHIE. What's what?

(**LIZZIE** *sighs, in a dramatic display of resignation, and takes the letter from wherever* **RUTHIE** *hid it.*)

LIZZIE. I'll take that.

RUTHIE. Don't

(**LIZZIE** *reads the letter.* **RUTHIE** *looks very upset by this.* **HANNAH** *stops cleaning and stares at both of them.*)

(**LIZZIE** *takes her time. She does not display any reaction.*)

(*She puts the letter in her pocket, continues chopping vegetables.*)

(**RUTHIE** *looks near tears.*)

(**HANNAH** *shakes her head and continues cleaning.*)

(*blackout*)

5. Allow Me First To Tell You Of Myself

(Kitchen #1, later. Everything is now more or less clean. The repaired Schiller bust sits on the kitchen table.)

*(**MARNIE** uncorks and pours wine, while **STUART** sits at the kitchen table, showing his sketches to **AUNT SYLVIA**.)*

*(**AUNT SYLVIA** has prosthetic hooks in place of her hands. With one hook, she eats cheez balls from a large cardboard cylinder with a sort of mathematical rigor.)*

(Outside, there are vestiges of the rainstorm in New Jersey.)

STUART. …So the thing is, the rights elapsed to this superhero who was last published in, uh, most people consider to the official run to have ended in 1947, except for this one-shot in 1963, from Dell Publishing, it was a very, uh, it's rare, it was printed so cheaply that most of them fell apart, the color separations were, they were terrible, American Male was either hot pink or bright yellow in most of the, uh, and it was only made available as part of a special promotion with Two Guys Stores.

AUNT SYLVIA. I remember Two Guys.

STUART. *(overlapping at the *)* Right. So we *heard that the rights elapsed.

AUNT SYLVIA. *(overlapping at the *)* *Marnie do you remember Two Guys?

MARNIE. I worked there when Stuart was a baby.

AUNT SYLVIA. Remember there was that one time when you urinated on the floor and on all of the new clothes Ma was getting us?

MARNIE. No.

AUNT SYLVIA. You were very upset. It was upsetting. Or maybe that was Lizzie. No it was you. You were standing in the cart and Ma had gotten all of this stuff and she got me a school dress and you peed on it. And they made her buy all the clothes because you peed on them.

MARNIE. They did not make us buy the clothes.

AUNT SYLVIA. Yes they did. They made us buy the clothes.

MARNIE. No they didn't. You and ma said they were going to do that but they didn't.

AUNT SYLVIA. *(to* **STUART***)* She's remembering it wrong.

MARNIE. No I'm not Sylvia.

AUNT SYLVIA. Whatever.

(brief awkward silence)

STUART. So we bought the rights – are you familiar with this, do you know what that means? To buy the rights to something, like a character?

AUNT SYLVIA. I'm not stupid.

STUART. Sorry.

AUNT SYLVIA. I've been swimming lately.

STUART. *(overlapping at the *)* Uh, right, I've been talking to, my friend Dipal is, he's a venture capitalist, and I really, I have this deeply held belief that graphic fiction is the art form of the future, so we decided *to revive the –

MARNIE. *(overlapping at the *)* *OK, Stuart, we don't really want to hear any more about the superheroes.

STUART. I was just.

MARNIE. Enough.

(Silence. **AUNT SYLVIA** *crunches cheez balls.* **MARNIE** *drinks.)*

Why don't you clean up?

STUART. I did clean up.

MARNIE. I need your help today. Will you please just help me with this one thing?

STUART. But I did. I cleaned up, look around.

*(***MARNIE** *holds back tears.)*

MARNIE. Stuart can you please come here for a second so I can talk to you?

STUART. OK.

(He deflates, goes to her.)

MARNIE. *(through her teeth)* What do you think you're doing?

STUART. *(overlapping at the *)* Nothing. I was just showing Aunt Sylvia my *character sketches –

MARNIE. *(overlapping at the *)* *Are you going to be on my side today?

STUART. Yes.

(overlapping at the *)

I'm on your side. OK? I cleaned up *already –

MARNIE. *(overlapping at the *)* *Do you swear?

STUART. Sure.

MARNIE. I want you to swear.

STUART. Really?

MARNIE. …

STUART. I swear.

(STUART pretends to clean the kitchen.)

MARNIE. Thank you, Stuart.

(AUNT SYLVIA munches.)

AUNT SYLVIA. Hey where is Ronald?

(no answer)

Where is Ronald? Is he coming?

MARNIE. I told you in the car.

AUNT SYLVIA. I don't think I was listening.

MARNIE. Stuart, will you please tell your Aunt where your father is?

AUNT SYLVIA. Why can't you tell me?

STUART. They're separated.
He's living in Philadelphia with a bunch of art students I introduced him to.

(more to MARNIE)

He's having a good time. They really like him.

AUNT SYLVIA. Oh.

STUART. Yeah.

AUNT SYLVIA. Doesn't he love you anymore?

MARNIE. I asked him to leave.

Don't spoil your appetite.

AUNT SYLVIA. I'm not.

MARNIE. We're leaving soon, Lizzie will freak out if you fill up on junk.

AUNT SYLVIA. Hey Stuart do you know what? We used to have Uncle Scrooge.

STUART. Uncle Scrooge is great.

MARNIE. Stuart, don't encourage her.

STUART. Carl Barks was an underrated genius.

MARNIE. Stuart.

(Silence. **AUNT SYLVIA** *munches.)*

AUNT SYLVIA. God is unbounded in His miracles.

Do you know God?

STUART. Me?

AUNT SYLVIA. Either of you.

STUART. I know of him.

AUNT SYLVIA. The lady with the Bibles came and put us all in a minivan and took us to the little beige church. I didn't want to go because there were too many coloreds but they made me and I went up and did the thing with the people. I gave my soul to Jesus.

STUART. It's really not polite to say coloreds anymore Aunt Sylvia.

(Silence; **AUNT SYLVIA** *munches,* **MARNIE** *drinks,* **STUART** *fake-cleans.)*

AUNT SYLVIA. Except I used to think we were Jewish. Am I Jewish?

MARNIE. You're not really anything Sylvia.

(to **STUART**, *re: her husband)*

He's having a good time? Did you talk to him?

STUART. You know. The kids seem to like him. All his stories.

AUNT SYLVIA. Ever since I let Jesus into my heart the changeling doesn't visit me anymore.

MARNIE. Well that's great for him.

AUNT SYLVIA. It used to always show up at very inconvenient times and it would tell me stuff in German mostly and drink all my soda and make a terrible mess.

STUART. Wait, what?

AUNT SYLVIA. Marnie, remember the changeling? Spanish Mary, we called it. Or sometimes just Maria. I don't know why we called it Spanish when it was German.

MARNIE. There wasn't any changeling. You were just ill.

AUNT SYLVIA. They gave me all kinds of medication, the shock treatments, everything, and it wouldn't leave me alone but then I accepted Jesus into my heart and it left me alone.

STUART. It spoke German?

AUNT SYLVIA. I think it was German. I didn't understand it, I don't know German.

STUART. Grandpa spoke German.

AUNT SYLVIA. That's right

MARNIE. Sylvia stop eating junk food.

AUNT SYLVIA. It would make a mess with my soda. Oh, and it also said, hep hep hep hep hep, just like that.

MARNIE. Sylvia, please, you're going to spoil your appetite and Lizzie is going to freak out.

(**AUNT SYLVIA** *eats, recalcitrant.*)

AUNT SYLVIA. Oh and it always wore a smock.

MARNIE. Sylvia give me those SYLVIA!

AUNT SYLVIA. NO! MINE!

(*They struggle over the cheez balls.* **AUNT SYLVIA** *makes whining noises.*)

STUART. Mom, come on, what are you. Mom.

(*He noncommittally tries to pull his mother off of his aunt. Cheez balls fly everywhere.*)

(beat)

AUNT SYLVIA. *(sad)* I'm hungry.

(brief unbearable pause)

MARNIE. I don't want Grandma's birthday to be depressing this year. Every year it's depressing and this year I want everyone to team up and make it not depressing.

(No answer. **MARNIE** *looks as if she might cry.)*

(brief unbearable pause)

Who's driving?

STUART. I think I should drive.

MARNIE. Not my Beemer.

STUART. We can take my car.

MARNIE. Did you clean it out like I asked?

STUART. When did you ask?

MARNIE. I'll drive.

STUART. You've had a lot of wine.

*(**MARNIE** stares daggers at **STUART**. Then, with an abrupt vicious glee:)*

MARNIE. *(a mocking, drunken falsetto)* "I love you, Mom!" Remember that story.

STUART. Yes.

MARNIE. *(to* **STUART***)* Not you. Sylvia.

AUNT SYLVIA. I'm hungry.

MARNIE. We had just gotten home and this car pulls into the driveway, and this middle-aged man reaches into the passenger side and pulls Stuart out by the scruff of his neck, and Stuart is just covered in puke, and then tosses him onto the lawn and drives off.

STUART. I don't think Sylvia needs to hear this story.

MARNIE. And we dragged him upstairs and tossed him in the shower, clothes on and everything, and through the closed door we hear this drunken caterwaul, and I open the door a crack and he's crying, "I love you, Mom! I love you, Mom!"

(She laughs.)

STUART. I think we should get going.

MARNIE. Who's driving?

STUART. *(overlapping at the *)* I don't care. Do you want me to clean out my car so we can *take it?

MARNIE. *(overlapping at the *)* *I'm driving but if Sylvia's taking those cheez doodles, we're taking your car. I am not getting that orange gunk all over the upholstery I just had cleaned.

STUART. Fine we'll take my car.

MARNIE. Ugh, your car's a sty.

*(Beat. **STUART** aggressively takes a huge handful of cheez balls and stuffs his mouth with them. He gets a little too close to **MARNIE** and chews with his mouth open, getting orange stuff all over himself and the immediate area.)*

(He takes a deep breath, exits.)

*(**MARNIE** breaks down, crying.)*

*(**AUNT SYLVIA** deftly takes a stubbed-out cigarette from a pocket or purse and places it in one of her prosthetic hooks.)*

What are you doing?

Uch, that's what smells like an ashtray, I thought it was just you.

That's disgusting, Sylvia, what do you think you're doing? You can't smoke in here.

AUNT SYLVIA. I'm just holding it.

MARNIE. It stinks. Throw it away. Please.

AUNT SYLVIA. I'll put it away if I can have my cheez balls.

MARNIE. I don't have them Stuart took them.

AUNT SYLVIA. I just want to hold it.

*(A tableau. **MARNIE** sobs, **AUNT SYLVIA** pretends to smoke.)*

(blackout)

6. Shameless Gossips, Swapping Stories

(Kitchen #2. The storm rages outside, more wind than rain.)

(The kitchen is empty. Off, we hear the inchoate noises of a too-loud TV set. It's just loud enough to be really annoying, but not loud enough for us to make out what's being said. There is, however, a laugh track. It makes the kitchen seem lonely.)

(Off, **LIZZIE** *shouts something we can't understand.)*

(beat)

LIZZIE. *(O.S.)* I SAID WHERE ARE YOU GOING?

RUTHIE. *(O.S.)* I CAN'T HEAR YOU OVER THE TELEVISION

(The TV goes off.)

LIZZIE. *(O.S.)* WHERE ARE YOU GOING?

RUTHIE. *(O.S.)* You don't have to yell. That television is too loud. No wonder we're all deaf.

LIZZIE. *(O.S.)* Well it's off now. Where are you going?

(beat)

Where are you going, sit down.

RUTHIE. *(O.S.)* I want some more Diet Sprite.

LIZZIE. *(O.S.)* Sit down.

RUTHIE. *(O.S.)* I'm thirsty

LIZZIE. *(O.S.)* Sit. Hannah'll get it HANNAH!

RUTHIE. *(O.S.)* Don't yell, I can get it

LIZZIE. *(O.S.)* HANNAH
HANNAH

HANNAH. *(O.S.)* What I'm right here what

LIZZIE. *(O.S.)* Grandma wants a Diet Sprite. Please.

RUTHIE. *(O.S.)* I can get it.

LIZZIE. *(O.S.)* Ma, sit down, what the fuck.

(The TV comes on again.)

(**RUTHIE** *says something we can't hear.*)

LIZZIE. *(O.S.)* WHAT?

(The TV goes off.)

What?

RUTHIE. *(O.S.)* You don't always have to use that language.

(No answer. The TV comes on again. Laugh track.)

(**HANNAH** *enters the kitchen. She starts to pour some soda.*)

(The **SHAPESHIFTER** *silently appears behind her. It is in the shape of* **STUART**.*)*

(He grabs the bottom of the soda bottle and abruptly jerks it upward, causing the soda to spill.)

HANNAH. *(startled)* What?

Stuart, what the fuck?

SHAPESHIFTER/STUART. Hep hep hep hep!

HANNAH. When did you get here?

Jesus Christ, you are such a jerk, I just washed this floor.

SHAPESHIFTER/STUART. Your eloquence has always brought me trouble.

HANNAH. You're not funny.

(He touches her face, invasive but not rough.)

Knock it off, Stuart.

SHAPESHIFTER/STUART. There is wisdom in the old traditions.

HANNAH. Get OFF I said

SHAPESHIFTER/STUART. *(barking)* Do not avoid the subject!

(This scares her – she is not used to **STUART** *disobeying her.)*

HANNAH. What are you. Doing.

(He traces one finger around one of her breasts. She sharply draws in breath.)

Stuart, stop.

SHAPESHIFTER/STUART. I only shrink from secret bloody murder

(She slaps his hand away but it doesn't work.)

HANNAH. Stuart knock it off we're not fucking kids anymore OK

STUART. STOP IT

(He gets even closer. She pushes him away but he looms over her.)

HANNAH. Please

(He pulls talcum powder from his smock and blows it at her. She coughs.)

(Something happens.)

*(The **SHAPESHIFTER** has now taken the form of **RUTHIE**.)*

…Grandma?

*(Unlike the real Ruthie, the **SHAPESHIFTER** is nimble and energetic.)*

SHAPESHIFTER/RUTHIE. Oh
What is so like it is what is this
To dance in the skin of one so far along
The heart sags it is
Feel
The world will not be fooled

HANNAH. Grandma what's happening

*(The **SHAPESHIFTER** drinks soda and does a little dance.)*

SHAPESHIFTER/RUTHIE. Oh it is what
This dance of skin and always many holes
She is so afraid this one is not lovely like you Oh Her veins are so nice and hard
Hep hep hep hep! She says don't oscillate, you might get a venereal disease on the upholstery
Oh but Something is something to say in the nightmare language to the pretty one

It says to say Oh watch me win the praise of angels
Come hold my hand girl come

HANNAH. What's going on

(*The* **SHAPESHIFTER** *takes her hand.*)

SHAPESHIFTER/RUTHIE. Feel
This one is so afraid Because she will end soon and all she knows is be alone
Somewhere is a forgotten sensation an echo of love leavened by vicissitude
You will have to excuse me the language of the sticky ones is not my language
Hep hep hep hep!
But what was I going to say, oh listen to me I am more facile by the second in a moment I will become her, she will vanish, I will lose all memory of what I am. Perhaps I will think I am dead, even though I can not die, and I will be buried, and I will use my transmutational legerdemain to pretend to decompose, and forget, I will forget, I will lie in the dirt in the cast of this old woman's skeleton and then in the cast of the dirt itself.

HANNAH. I don't understand.

SHAPESHIFTER/RUTHIE. When the secrets accumulate in the corners of the houses of the wretched sticky ones, and are moved from house to house in boxes and are buried under porches and hidden in cabinets and toilet tanks, those secrets amass into a sort of varmint, oh Hannah, I do not want to become this old woman, how I would like to take the shape of your desires and imbibe the sweet and sticky liquid don't mind if I do

(*She takes the soda from* **HANNAH** *and downs it.*)

Thank you.
But I do not want to become indelible, so I must tell you what it is I came to tell you and then it's back to the German and the lightning and the enigmatic flummadiddle.

SHAPESHIFTER/RUTHIE. *(cont.)* An epistle circulates, it is pink, and scented, like the musky perfume worn on the back of a soft white neck when you were a girl. Find the message and something will bump. But I can feel my joints stiffening, tendons shrinking, I must go, I must go, I must go.
Poof.

(Something happens.)

(The **SHAPESHIFTER** *is gone. Except for the spilled soda, everything is back to normal.)*

*(***LIZZIE** *enters.)*

LIZZIE. What happened?

HANNAH. *(dazed)* I don't know. I mean what do you mean?

LIZZIE. Is Stuart here?

HANNAH. What?

LIZZIE. You yelled Stuart's name and then it sounded like you fell.

(beat)

HANNAH. I think. The wind. Must have scared me.
Hey.
Do you smell that?

LIZZIE. Smell what.

HANNAH. It's the perfume I used to wear. When I was like 14.

LIZZIE. I don't smell anything.
Grandma wants her soda.

HANNAH. What's in your pocket?

LIZZIE. What's what.

HANNAH. Grandma had it before. She was trying to hide it from me.

LIZZIE. It's just an old letter. It's private.

HANNAH. Why's Grandma so freaked out about it?

LIZZIE. Grandma's freaked out about everything.

HANNAH. Can I read it?

LIZZIE. It's private.

HANNAH. Why does it smell like my old perfume?

LIZZIE. It doesn't smell like anything.

HANNAH. I want to read it.

LIZZIE. No.

HANNAH. Give it to me.

(She goes for it. There's a small, brief struggle.)

LIZZIE. Hannah, what the fuck?

HANNAH. Come on, Mom.

*(**RUTHIE** hobbles in, with her walker again.)*

RUTHIE. What's the matter?

HANNAH. Nothing.

LIZZIE. Nothing.

HANNAH. I just thought I heard Stuart, and it scared me, but it was just the wind. Here's your soda, I'm sorry it took so long.

LIZZIE. I'm going back to see how it ends.

HANNAH. Mom, wait.

*(**LIZZIE** exits.)*

*(**HANNAH** and **RUTHIE** are left alone.)*

RUTHIE. It's my birthday.

HANNAH. I know.

I'm sorry.

Happy birthday.

RUTHIE. I wasn't even really thinking about it myself. I think I just forgot about it.

I was just thirsty.

HANNAH. Sorry. I got distracted.

I thought I saw something.

(A moment. They assess each other.)

…Do you feel like something's going on? Like something weird.

RUTHIE. Not.

Not particularly.

HANNAH. No.

No, I guess not.

(silence)

Well uh. Well I have to Uh I have to finish my emails. Happy birthday.

(indicating the other room)

Do you need help uh

RUTHIE. No.

I'm going to sit in here.

I don't really like that show.

HANNAH. OK uh

Happy uh

Happy birthday

(HANNAH *exits.)*

(RUTHIE *looks out the window, scared.)*

(The wind kicks up.)

(blackout)

7. A Discreet Disease

(Kitchen #2. The whole family is crowded in the kitchen. **LIZZIE** *is hustling to get the food out to the [offstage] dining room.* **RUTHIE, AUNT SYLVIA,** *and* **STUART** *sit around the kitchen table, crowded with soda, snacks, and hors'douvres of various kinds.)*

*(***HANNAH** *and* **MARNIE** *stand or sit as is expedient.)*

(Throughout the following, **AUNT SYLVIA** *eats hors' douvres recklessly, with abandon, table manners be damned. The cigarette butt is still in one of her hooks. All are clearly disgusted by this, except* **STUART,** *who munches obliviously.)*

STUART. *(overlapping at the *)* So I'm trying to add this sort of quasi-ironic layer of literary* references –

MARNIE. *(overlapping at the *)* *Do you need help? Lizzie, do you need help?

LIZZIE. I'm fine.

STUART. *(overlapping at the *)* There are actually, there's a newfound respect for graphic novels as an *art form.

MARNIE. *(overlapping at the *)* *Lizzie you don't have to do it all yourself.

LIZZIE. I'm fine. How much did you say you paid for this superhero?

STUART. It's not – The bulk of it is being handled by Dipal, do you remember Dipal?

AUNT SYLVIA. Like the University?

STUART. No, that's, it's spelled differently, that's his name, he's from India originally. My high school friend? Anyway, he made a lot of money in the dot-com thing, he's like this venture capitalist, anyway, he wanted to break into the entertainment industry, so.

LIZZIE. So how much did he pay for it?

STUART. I don't, uh. Like seven-fifty?

LIZZIE. Dollars?

STUART. Seven hundred and fifty thousand.

LIZZIE. Jesus.

STUART. Actually it's a steal.

RUTHIE. Your grandfather used to like comic books on the toilet, he had The Shadow, I think, and Gasoline Alley, and he used to love Doonesbury, that was during Nixon, but we just threw most of them away.

STUART. Well this is more of an intellectual property thing.

LIZZIE. And what is he? Captain America?

STUART. *(overlapping at the *)* American Male, he's called, it's a little more obscure, the rights *had lapsed –

LIZZIE. *(overlapping at the *)* *Isn't that the catalog, like the fag clothing catalogue?

HANNAH. That's what I said too.

MARNIE. The what?

HANNAH. It's like this catalog full of faggy clothes, like see-through mesh shirts and like penis hammocks and stuff.

RUTHIE. A penis what? What are we talking about?

STUART. *(overlapping at the *)* No, that's the International Male catalog, and it's *not –

MARNIE. *(overlapping at the *)* *How do you know what the catalog's called?

HANNAH. Stuart's a fag!

RUTHIE. Is Stuart a homosexual?

STUART. No, Grandma, and I would prefer, you know, there are a lot of people who find the term "fag" pretty offensive.

LIZZIE. Lighten up, Stuart. The term "fag catalog" totally came from my gay guy friend.

RUTHIE. Stuart, are you gay?

HANNAH. Of course not, just look at him. He's not even, like, a metrosexual.

RUTHIE. It's fine if you are. It's none of anybody's business.

MARNIE. We always did think you were a "little light in the loafers." Right?

RUTHIE. What is that smell, who's smoking? Ugh, Sylvia, you're disgusting.

AUNT SYLVIA. What?

RUTHIE. Throw that cigarette away!

AUNT SYLVIA. I'm not smoking, I know Lizzie doesn't want us smoking in her "fancy" house. I'm just saving it.

RUTHIE. You're going to get ashes in the dip!

AUNT SYLVIA. It's not even lit, Ma!

MARNIE. She's right, Sylvia, what did I tell you? That thing stunk up the car and it's stinking up the whole kitchen. Just put it in an ashtray or something.

HANNAH. I think we threw out all the ashtrays. Mom, do we have any ashtrays?

LIZZIE. *(a "not my problem" gesture)* ...

MARNIE. Just throw it out. How much do cigarettes cost? We'll stop at a gas station and buy you some Pall Malls.

AUNT SYLVIA. Kents.

MARNIE. It doesn't matter.

(Silence. AUNT SYLVIA eats, defiant.)

RUTHIE. Uch, look at that. I would say I can't believe it but it's Sylvia so I can believe anything. Look at her, she's a disgrace, making a mess out of everything, no one else wants to eat, well no wonder! You're spoiling everyone's appetite!

STUART. Grandma.

RUTHIE. Look at her! Look at that mess, food all over the table, all down her front, it's disgusting! You're disgusting, Sylvia, I'm ashamed that you're my daughter.

LIZZIE. Jesus, ma, take a fucking pill.

MARNIE. She's right, Lizzie. Sylvia has to learn.

(Silence. HANNAH and STUART share a look.)

AUNT SYLVIA. It's really hard to eat when you don't have any hands.

MARNIE. We understand that, Sylvia. It's not about your prostheses, we all know that's not your fault. It's about your behavior, and the cigarette, and it's about learning to have consideration for the people around you.

(long awful silence)

HANNAH. Mom, you want some help?

(She goes to help.)

LIZZIE. What are you doing, stop that, no one knows how I want it done. What are you doing?

HANNAH. …

LIZZIE. Fucking fine, whatever, OK? But I want everyone to know that none of you can blame me when everything gets fucked up.

STUART. I can help too.

LIZZIE & HANNAH. No.

STUART. Hannah, you want to go out for a ride or something? Like take a ride out to the store or something?

HANNAH. What for?

STUART. Just go out for, for a ride, you know, catch up?

HANNAH. We catch up all the time. You call me like twice a week.

MARNIE. He just wants to be alone with you.

STUART. *(to MARNIE, resentful)* I thought I was supposed to be gay.

RUTHIE. I'm proud of you no matter what, Stuart.

MARNIE. *(stage-whisper)* (Why are you being so hostile today!)

STUART. (I'm not being hostile!)

MARNIE. *(full voice)* If you didn't want to see Grandma then you should've just stayed home!

STUART. What? Who said I…
What?

(AUNT SYLVIA, seeing her chance, goes back to devouring hors'douvres.)

RUTHIE. STOP IT STOP IT STOP IT! You are disgusting like an animal!

(silence)

STUART. Sylvia, do you want me to uh. I mean I can fix you a plate if you uh.

MARNIE. She needs to learn how to do things for herself.

AUNT SYLVIA. I'm older than you are Marnie. I'm the oldest.

MARNIE. Then you should know better.

(She takes the platter away.)

AUNT SYLVIA. What are you doing?

STUART. Mom, come on.

MARNIE. Dinner's almost ready.

AUNT SYLVIA. I'm not as bad as I used to be you know. I accepted Jesus into my heart and now the changeling doesn't visit anymore like it used to.

RUTHIE. You can't accept Jesus into your heart. We're Jewish.

AUNT SYLVIA. *(to MARNIE)* I thought you said I wasn't anything.

MARNIE. You're not.

RUTHIE. Marnie, have you gained weight? I don't remember your derriere being that big.

MARNIE. What? I don't know.

RUTHIE. *(laughs)* I remember it being big but not that big. But who knows, my memory is so terrible these days. I remember we were. Was somebody gay?

STUART. It was just a joke, Grandma, we were joking around.

RUTHIE. Oh.

What were we talking about?

STUART. I bought a superhero. American Male.

RUTHIE. You used to love superheroes. You had all the dolls.

STUART. I still do!

RUTHIE. Remember that time you and Hannah were playing and Hannah broke them all?

STUART. *(this is a bitter memory)* Yes.

(beat)

But these are different ones, I mean they're the same ones, but different actual dolls. I bought them vintage off eBay, you know eBay?

AUNT SYLVIA. I know eBay. That's the website.

RUTHIE. Uch, I hate computers.

(*LIZZIE enters.*)

LIZZIE. It's soup.

(*They all get up to leave.*)

MARNIE. (I need you today.)

STUART. (OK!)

Grandma, do you need help?

RUTHIE. Thank you, Stuart.

(*He helps her up.*)

STUART. Hey, Grandma, I wanted to ask you. Grandpa was into translation, right? Like he would try and translate stuff from German and Russian.

RUTHIE. It was just a hobby, he never did anything with it. He never had any ambition, your grandfather.

STUART. Do you remember anything about it? Like did you save any of the stuff he was working on?

(*tiny beat*)

RUTHIE. Oh that's all thrown away now. It was so boring, he used to go on and on about it and I would tell him, no one wants to hear about that stuff! But he didn't care. The only thing we kept was that Beethoven statue and that was just because you wanted it.

STUART. It was Schiller.

RUTHIE. Who was?

STUART. Schiller, the statue. Never mind

So. You having a good birthday so far?

RUTHIE. I've had worse.

(*They all file out. LIZZIE scuttles back and forth, getting things to the table.*)

Who moved the fucking hors'douvres?

(*No answer. She exits, re-enters. Beat.*)

LIZZIE. Stuart, could you help me in here with this please?

HANNAH. *(O.S.)* I can get it!

LIZZIE. No, I need Stuart!

STUART. *(O.S.)* Just a second!

(*Perhaps a long beat as* **STUART** *helps* **RUTHIE** *sit offstage.*)

(**LIZZIE** *takes the pink envelope from her hiding place.*)

STUART. Hey what's up.

(*She presents him the envelope.*)

LIZZIE. If you insist on holding on to this then you need to be careful with it.

STUART. Where did you get this?

LIZZIE. Grandma had it.

You should probably just throw it away.

STUART. I was keeping it in the bust of Schiller.

LIZZIE. That means nothing to me.

STUART. Grandpa's bust of Schiller? That I took when he died?

LIZZIE. …

STUART. Um, I saw something, there was something kind of weird.

HANNAH. *(O.S.)* You guys OK in there?

LIZZIE. Fine!

(*loudly, for* **HANNAH**'s *benefit*)

Stuart, can you grab the end of this?

(*She hands him one end of a small dish, one that obviously does not need two people to carry it.*)

STUART. I was on the phone with Hannah. But then while I was still on the phone with her, I saw her, right in front of me. Except she was speaking in German, I think, and. She was behaving very strangely.

LIZZIE. OK, Stuart, everyone's hungry.

STUART. She smashed the bust open and then took the letter and then disappeared in a cloud.

LIZZIE. *(fake laugh)* You sound like Aunt Sylvia.

(*They exit, carrying the absurdly small dish.*)

(*Lights change.*)

8. Judge! Make The Right Time Come

(Kitchen #2 later. Dinner has happened, off, and we hear muted conversation.)

(HANNAH enters. She takes a large birthday cake from the fridge and begins planting birthday candles in it, as chatter continues off.)

(LIZZIE enters.)

LIZZIE. You OK in here?

HANNAH. I'm fine.

(LIZZIE watches her.)

HANNAH. I'm fine, I can do it, sit down! You're such a control freak!

LIZZIE. Oh piss off I'm not a control freak.

(But she does not stop.)

HANNAH. Will you please go sit down?

(LIZZIE exits. Beat.)

(STUART enters.)

STUART. Hi.

HANNAH. I'm fine.

STUART. What?

HANNAH. I don't need any help.

STUART. OK.

(beat)

HANNAH. You want something?

STUART. I just wanted. To talk about.
Is Rocco coming over?

HANNAH. Fuck Rocco.

STUART. What's the matter.

HANNAH. He's a dick, I don't want to talk about it.
What is that smell?

STUART. What?

HANNAH. I keep smelling this like perfume. From when I was like in middle school.

(He produces the pink envelope.)

What is that?

STUART. It's the letter You wrote me.

HANNAH. What letter.

STUART. When we were in middle school.

HANNAH. Stuart…I don't think it's really healthy to keep obsessing over that time, ya know? I mean, kids fuck around, but we're not kids. I mean, there are sound genetic reasons for the incest taboo. I don't want my kids all retarded and shit.

STUART. Who said anything about kids?

HANNAH. Whatever, Stuart, it's also fucking pretty gross.

(By now he is standing too close to her.)

HANNAH. What are you doing?

STUART. You want me to read it to you?

HANNAH. I never wrote you a letter, it was all over by the time we got to middle school, and please back off you're a little too close to me.

STUART. I used to read this every night before I went to bed.

(quiet)

Sometimes I would masturbate six, seven, times in a row.

HANNAH. Stuart, you are creeping me out.

STUART. I would read it over and over again, how you thought of me, and what you would do with the hairbrush. I would think about you on your bed, on your stomach, your teeth clenched and I would think I was dreaming this, it couldn't possibly be real.

HANNAH. That's because it wasn't real.

Look Stuart, I never wrote any fucking letter, I had a real boyfriend by the time I was 12 and I was over this shit, you should get over it too –

(He tries to kiss her.)

HANNAH. *(cont.)* Stuart knock it off what the fuck are you doing –

(She shoves a handful of icing in his face.)

Jesus Christ –

STUART. I'm sorry

(LIZZIE enters. HANNAH quickly palms the letter.)

LIZZIE. What happened?

HANNAH. Nothing

STUART. I fell.

LIZZIE. Jesus Christ, look at this mess. Are you retarded?

STUART. It's my fault.

LIZZIE. I'll just.

(takes a look at the cake, determines it's hopeless)

Just bring it out there.

(HANNAH goes to light the candles.)

Don't light it in here, light it out there.

Stuart hang out a minute.

(HANNAH takes the cake out, exasperated.)

LIZZIE. I don't know why you bother.

STUART. …

LIZZIE. You shouldn't try to talk about it with her.

STUART. I know.

LIZZIE. She's in denial. She'll never acknowledge it.

(STUART starts to cry a little.)

Sh. Come here.

(She holds him.)

You need to move on.

STUART. I know. It's stupid. I just.

LIZZIE. Sh,

(They kiss on the mouth. It's a deep, long kiss.)

(They break.)

(beat)

LIZZIE. We should uh.

STUART. Yeah.

(They exit. Perhaps strains of "happy birthday" are heard off.)

End Act One

ACT TWO

9. Another Terror At That Time

(Music: something languid, sad, hallucinogenic.)

(Kitchen #1. It is about eight months later, the middle of the night. It is very dark. **STUART** *stumbles in, fumbling, carrying something large, perhaps knocking stuff over. He turns an overhead light on; the light is stark and just illuminates the table. Something about it makes the room look even darker.* **STUART** *wears a rumpled dark suit. He looks like shit.)*

(He holds the Schiller bust, a portfolio, and collapsible table top easel. He futzes around for a moment, setting it up, perhaps putting a clip light on the easel, making the light even starker.)

(Before working, he stares at Schiller. Schiller appears to stare back at him.)

(He draws. As he draws, he speaks some of the dialogue of the comic he's drawing.)

STUART. "American Male! And so I see your face again."
"Yes, Masha, we were to meet again."
"God, you have come – "
"To say a last farewell."

(He draws, mumbles, perhaps uttering sound effects of a superhero fight the way a kid might. He stops.)

(He rifles through a cabinet or pantry, stares for a while at the less-than-satisfactory options. He settles on an ridiculously enormous bucket of Teddy Grahams of the kind found at one of those wholesale bulk places. He stuffs his face with Teddy Grahams and draws and makes fight noises for as long as can be endured.)

(*At some point,* **AUNT SYLVIA** *skulks into the room, unseen by* **STUART**. *She wears a shortish robe that perhaps reveals a little too much. She holds a few sheets of paper. She watches* **STUART** *work.*)

(*long beat*)

(*She undoes her robe with her hooks. We may or may not see her exposed body.*)

(**STUART** *is oblivious.*)

AUNT SYLVIA. (*quiet*) I quit smoking

STUART. (*startled*) What

(*sees her*)

AA!

Sylvia what are you doing.

AUNT SYLVIA. I heard someone come in and I thought it was you so I came down to be with you.

STUART. OK Sylvia could you please close your robe please?

AUNT SYLVIA. Why?

STUART. It's just it's a little inappropriate, it's OK just please it's making me very uncomfortable.

AUNT SYLVIA. What if I don't want to.

STUART. Just please.

AUNT SYLVIA. They all used to think I was the beautiful one. Not Lizzie. I was Daddy's favorite. He would read to me in German or Russian, sometimes Yiddish, I think he spoke some Yiddish too. Also some Lithuanian. Imagine that? Almost five languages and just a bus driver.

Ma didn't like it because Daddy liked me better than her.

STUART. OK.

AUNT SYLVIA. When I was young Jerry Weissman would come over, Paulette's older brother, he was in the Air Force, and I would catch him looking at my chest.

STUART. OK I'm sure you were very beautiful but you have to put your clothes back on Sylvia.

AUNT SYLVIA. I remember once I was at Paulette's and I was daydreaming, maybe I fell asleep, I liked it over there. The changeling wouldn't follow me there and I would look at the pictures of Jerry in his uniform.

She used to have this thing she did where she pretended to feel bad for me because we were too poor to afford a swimming pool but really it was to make me feel bad, and I wanted to hold her at the bottom of the pool and watch the air bubbles float out of her mouth while I held her against the blue rubber floor but.

Actually what I really wanted was for her and me to get together and do that to someone else maybe Lizzie sometimes maybe your mother maybe that poor other girl, the one with the.

Missing hands or.

But that's me.

You were always so nice to me, Stuart, I always thought if you were going to pick one of us it would be me, but no, it's always Lizzie. I always wanted to hold you and they said no, or if they did say yes they would watch me really close, like what was I going to do, break your neck? Hold his head, Ma would always yell at me, but I said I know, I know that's what you're supposed to do with babies, I said I had a cat, didn't I, I knew how to take care of soft gentle things.

STUART. Uh

Sylvia, will you please get dressed.

AUNT SYLVIA. I am a person, you know. I have desire. I like to be touched. Will you touch me?

STUART. OK. OK, how about this. You close your robe and I'll give you a hug. OK?

AUNT SYLVIA. *(re: hooks, robe)* Will you help me?

STUART. I would. Rather not.

(Beat. She ties her robe. She is pretty deft at tasks like this but it still takes some time and effort.)

(He hugs her.)

AUNT SYLVIA. Hope is cruel.

STUART. I know, it is.

AUNT SYLVIA. What are you drawing?

STUART. My comic.

AUNT SYLVIA. Oh, American Man?

STUART. American Male. Did you get the first issue? I sent it to you.

AUNT SYLVIA. I don't like those things, they're garish. I gave it to Momo.

(*beat*)

Did you ever think: why are we alive to see this?

STUART. See what? Grandma dying?

AUNT SYLVIA. That's not what I mean. The changeling hasn't been around in such a long time.

STUART. …

AUNT SYLVIA. Anyway Ma isn't dead. Not really.

STUART. Uh.

I'm sorry but she is.

AUNT SYLVIA. No, I'm not stupid don't talk to me like I'm stupid. Something else happened. With the changeling. It's like dying but it's much worse, you just fade, like a cloud, you evaporate and then you're not anywhere, you're sort of stuck in the changeling and the changeling's stuck in you, it's sort of complicated, I don't really think I understand it that much.

STUART. Sylvia, I think we should go to bed.

AUNT SYLVIA. No you think I should go to bed.

Can I have some Teddy Grahams?

(*He holds the bucket out to her. She eats, with her hooks. He eats. They eat.*)

When the changeling gets stuck in someone it's like when a flower slowly turns to face the sun, or when a swan turns around in the water. It's beautiful but also sort of terrible. It's not at all like death. When death happens, it's sudden, like lightning, like a jump.

I tried everything to get away from that changeling.

STUART. It isn't real.
AUNT SYLVIA. You've seen it don't lie to me.
STUART. ...
   Why do you think that?
AUNT SYLVIA. It told me.
STUART. Are you seeing it again?
AUNT SYLVIA. It faxed me.
STUART. What?
AUNT SYLVIA. Look.
   (Shows him the paper. He reads.)
   It used to be stupid, like an animal, but then it got smart. It spoke German back then, I think, but I don't think it knew what it was saying, it was just like when a dog barks. One day your mother came home from work at the Pergament and I stole her smock and put it on the changeling so I would always know it was the changeling and not Ma or Marnie or Lizzie or even sometimes it would be Jerry or Paulette. Or Daddy. But it was never Daddy, I don't think.
   I could always tell who it was when it started talking, or when it drank soda, it loves soda, but by that time I would sometimes already be in trouble.
STUART. It wrote this?
   ...
   And faxed it to you?
AUNT SYLVIA. It can't come near me now that I let Jesus in my heart so it sends me faxes. That's why I tried to kill myself on the railroad tracks, to get it to leave me alone, but it didn't work.
   Why did you pick Lizzie and not me?
STUART. I didn't pick her. I would um.
   Please don't talk about this with anyone.
AUNT SYLVIA. Everyone picks Lizzie and not me.
STUART. ...Am I going crazy?

AUNT SYLVIA. There's nothing crazy about it. Everyone saw the changeling. They just lied about it. I told the truth and they sent me away. They did things to me but I was never crazy.

(She rubs the side of his face with her hook. She rubs his chest with it.)

STUART. OK you have to stop that Aunt Sylvia.
You have to stop that or I will make you stop and I really do not want to do that.

(Beat. She stops.)

MARNIE. What are you two doing? Sylvia, what the hell are you wearing?

(MARNIE enters.)

STUART. Hi Mom. I'm on a deadline and we were just having a snack.

MARNIE. For god's sake Sylvia put some clothes on. Now.

(AUNT SYLVIA glares at her but acquiesces, exiting.)

MARNIE. *(to STUART)* You should go to bed. Grandma's funeral is tomorrow.

STUART. I'll be fine I just I have a deadline, I have to get this in.

MARNIE. What are you, going to messenger it over during the funeral? Go to bed, Stuart.

(beat)

STUART. Did you and Lizzie used to see any of the same things as Aunt Sylvia?

MARNIE. I'm not talking about this now.

STUART. Did you?

MARNIE. Good night. We're leaving at eight-thirty, no excuses.

(She exits. STUART draws and eats Teddy Grahams.)

(blackout)

10. The Bright Smiling Blade

(Kitchen #2, dawn, a few hours later on the same day. It's overcast, like the sky is about to burst.)

(HANNAH enters, dressed for the funeral. She is so furious that her hands are trembling. She tosses her keys on the table and makes coffee, slamming things around, stomping, and generally being louder than is necessary. She grabs a bowl from a cabinet and sets it on the table. She takes the perfumed pink letter from her purse, sets it on fire, and watches it burn.)

(A smoke detector goes off.)

(After a minute or so of this, LIZZIE comes downstairs, partially dressed for the funeral. She has been crying.)

LIZZIE. What the fuck?! What's burning?

(HANNAH gestures towards the bowl.)

What are you doing Are you fucking retarded? Put that out. Put that out I said, Jesus Christ.

(She goes to grab it, HANNAH pulls the bowl away.)

HANNAH. Let it burn. You see what that is? Let it burn.

(LIZZIE looks at it, glares at HANNAH with narrow eyes, goes to open a window. The smoke detector shrieks.)

LIZZIE. Jesus Christ.

(LIZZIE searches for the smoke detector, finds it, drags a chair over to the wall where it resides, yanks to off of the wall and removes the battery. This might take a while.)

(LIZZIE gets off the chair.)

(overlapping at the *)

I don't need this bullshit today, OK, Hannah, I am burying my goddamn mother *and I'm not listening to this.

HANNAH. *(overlapping at the * and **)* *Grandma read it. One of you lunatic assholes left it out at her birthday party and she read the thing, **she basically blamed me for killing her.

LIZZIE. *(overlapping at the **)* **I'm not listening to this.

HANNAH. She basically blamed me for killing her.

LIZZIE. What are you talking about?

HANNAH. She said I broke her heart.

LIZZIE. She did not say that.

HANNAH. Yes she did.

LIZZIE. *(overlapping at the *)* Well she didn't mean it. She said shit like that all the time. If she really was going to die because of something you did, *she would have died a long time ago.

HANNAH. *(overlapping at the *)* *Something someone else did –

LIZZIE. Look, your grandmother was not a child. Little kids fuck around sometimes, it's not the end of the world.

HANNAH. Did you do it?

LIZZIE. I didn't, do what.

HANNAH. You know what I'm talking about.

LIZZIE. Hannah.

It is a funeral. OK? First of all, you're being paranoid, I didn't do anything, second of all, it is a funeral, for your grandmother.

*(The **SHAPESHIFTER**, stuck in the form of **RUTHIE**, appears at the window. She is in the form of Ruthie's corpse, more or less, and looks it – she moves stiffly, and maybe looks a little like a zombie. They do not notice her.)*

HANNAH. Where did it come from then?

LIZZIE. I don't know Hannah maybe you wrote it and forgot.

HANNAH. Bullshit I did not write that.

LIZZIE. I am not talking about this with you. I just got off the phone with your father in San Diego, who is not even willing to get on a plane and come out for this, OK?

HANNAH. Can you blame him?

LIZZIE. Go fuck yourself.

(She exits. **HANNAH** *looks at the smoldering remains of the letter.)*

(She notices the **SHAPESHIFTER** *grinning at her through the window.)*

HANNAH. Oh God

(The **SHAPESHIFTER** *waves, stiffly.* **HANNAH** *is terrified but goes over to the window.)*

(a still moment)

(The **SHAPESHIFTER** *slaps the window,* **HANNAH** *jumps.)*

Oh!

(beat)

Grandma?

What the fuck.

(She opens the door. The **SHAPESHIFTER** *partially stumbles in.)*

SHAPESHIFTER/RUTHIE. Hep hep hep hep!

HANNAH. ...Grandma?

SHAPESHIFTER/RUTHIE. No not Großmutter, pretty one, but me, the varmint of cancerous conveniences, me made sticky, it's heartrending news, isn't it. I sat with the old-timey one, she coveted me, baited me with soda pop, that is what it's called yes, soda pop, also baited, this strange argot you sticky ones enjoy, and when I came to her she asked me to imbibe her form, to take her shape and Oh look at me now Oh. Look at what has come and bumped.

(beat)

HANNAH. OK.

I don't know what you are but you have to leave us alone. Today is my grandmother's funeral and if you go around reanimating her dead body or whatever you're going to make a lot of people very uncomfortable and this includes me.

SHAPESHIFTER/RUTHIE. Oh but she is not inert, we are buffaloed together, sticky like this.

*(She goes to kiss **HANNAH**.)*

HANNAH. Gross, what are you, STOP.

SHAPESHIFTER/RUTHIE. It's better with the soda pop.

It's sort of like this, where Großmutter is:

A staircase that descends to the great hall, the door is opened, you look inside, and – oh god! The walls are hung with black, and from the ground a scaffold rises, also draped in black, and in the center sits a block, pitch black, and next to it a stole. The hall is full of people pressed around the dreadful sculpture, awaiting, eyes alive with lust.

HANNAH. What do you want from me?

SHAPESHIFTER/RUTHIE. For now just some soda pop.

HANNAH. … Do you care what kind of soda it is?

SHAPESHIFTER/RUTHIE. Anything that is not diet.

*(**HANNAH** goes to the fridge, gets a bottle of Ginger Ale.)*

HANNAH. This OK?

SHAPESHIFTER/RUTHIE. Yes yes.

*(The **SHAPESHIFTER** greedily grabs the soda and guzzles it, spilling lots of it.)*

SHAPESHIFTER/RUTHIE. I am sorry about the mess.

HANNAH. It's OK.

Will you please go now?

SHAPESHIFTER/RUTHIE. Not until the privy place is open unto you all. Oh, but I shall hide and bear witness. Oh and there is also this:

Großmutter has sent me from her side. She wants to speak with you all one last time. Alone on earth.

*(**HANNAH** does not respond.)*

Hep hep hep hep!

*(The **SHAPESHIFTER** hobbles out the door, cheerful but for the rigor mortis. **HANNAH** stares.)*

(blackout)

11. My Strongest And Most Precious Casket

(Kitchens #1 and #2, merged again as in scene eight, that evening. The funeral has taken place, and all have gone home except for the immediate family. It's raining outside. Lots and lots of food sits out, and all pick at it absently, except **SYLVIA**, *who pointedly does not eat anything.)*

LIZZIE & MARNIE. *(O.S.) (ad lib as needed)* OK. OK, thanks, thank you. Thanks.

(etc.)

(They see the unseen guests out and come to the table. It is silent. All [except **SYLVIA**] *munch joylessly.*

LIZZIE. Well. That's that then I guess.

STUART. *(overlapping at the *)* Is there anything you *need?

LIZZIE. *(overlapping at the *)* *No.

(They sit, eat. **LIZZIE** *gets up, gets a bottle of cognac. She pours herself a very large glass.)*

Anybody want some?

*(***MARNIE** *raises her hand.* **LIZZIE** *pours a lot of cognac into her water glass.)*

MARNIE. Not that much.

LIZZIE. Really?

*(***LIZZIE** *guzzles it.* **MARNIE** *hesitates, guzzles hers.)*

STUART. I'll have some.

*(***LIZZIE** *pours him a lot of cognac. He tries to take a big sip, gags a little.)*

Jesus.

HANNAH. Don't be such a pussy, Stuart.

*(***HANNAH** *grabs the bottle and pours herself a big glass. They all drink, except for* **AUNT SYLVIA**.*)*

AUNT SYLVIA. I don't want any.

MARNIE. You can't have any anyway Sylvia.

(They drink. **AUNT SYLVIA** *pouts. After a beat,* **LIZZIE** *gets up and gets a sippie cup from a cabinet.)*

LIZZIE. You want like a mixer?

AUNT SYLVIA. Who? Me? I don't want any.

LIZZIE. I'll put some coke in it.

MARNIE. Lizzie what are you doing she can't drink. She's on medication.

LIZZIE. Oh shut up please Marnie.

AUNT SYLVIA. She's right I can't drink.

LIZZIE. Just pretend then.

(She hands **AUNT SYLVIA** *the sippie cup full of alcohol.* **SYLVIA** *takes a tentative sip, then spits it all over.* **HANNAH** *chokes back a laugh.)*

Jesus Sylvia.

MARNIE. You shouldn't be giving her booze, Lizzie.

AUNT SYLVIA. *(defiant)* No! I've drunk before. I'll drink.

STUART. Well cheers.

(He raises his glass. No one else does. They drink.)

(beat)

MARNIE. Anybody remember any funny stories about Grandma?

(silence)

AUNT SYLVIA. I have a story but it's not funny. Actually it's very sad.

MARNIE. No thank you Sylvia.

(pause)

I have one.

(pause)

Anyone want to hear it?

(pause)

STUART. Sure Mom.

MARNIE. Well first. Hannah, did you know your Aunt Sylvia dated a porno actor in the late 70s, early 80s?

LIZZIE. Stop it, Marnie.

HANNAH. You did?

AUNT SYLVIA. He was nice.

MARNIE. We were all sitting around the table, Grandma was going on and on about whatever thing, some buffet or something, and Sylvia brought this magazine, like a nudie magazine with her new boyfriend in it.

LIZZIE. It was a joke.

MARNIE. And in the centerfold is this large hairy man clutching his dong, with the fold and the staples right in the middle of it. This was not a classy magazine.

HANNAH. No kidding.

MARNIE. And we're passing it around the table, and someone passes it to grandma, I don't think she even knows what it is, and she's talking, talking, and suddenly she looks down at it, and whoomp! She shuts it and passes it on.

(*Only* **MARNIE** *laughs at this. They drink.*)

AUNT SYLVIA. (*to* **HANNAH**) That was right before I tried to kill myself.

MARNIE. Hey I have an idea.

Want to read Grandma's will?

LIZZIE. Right now?

STUART. I don't know if that's such a good idea.

MARNIE. I have it right here.

HANNAH. She didn't have anything, did she?

MARNIE. She had a little squirreled away.

LIZZIE. It all went to pay for the old age home.

MARNIE. It's not really the official will anyway, I think she had that drawn up years ago. Didn't she leave everything to Stuart? It's more like a note.

(*takes out a paper*)

She typed it. In all caps.

AUNT SYLVIA. I'd like to hear it.

LIZZIE. Don't.

MARNIE. *(reading)* WHATEVER I HAVE LEFT THAT THEY DIDN'T TAKE FROM ME I WANT TO DIVIDE EQUALLY BETWEEN YOU ALL.

LIZZIE. Marnie, stop.

MARNIE. It's in all caps that's why I'm yelling.

(reads) YOU CAN DIVIDE UP ALL MY CLOTHES.

ALL MY NICE DRESSES SHOULD MOSTLY GO TO LIZZIE AND HANNAH BECAUSE OF THEIR LOOKS.

SYLVIA CAN HAVE ALL MY KNIT PANTS THEY'RE VERY COMFORTABLE.

MARNIE CAN JUST HAVE WHATEVER'S LEFT INCLUDING ALSO MY KNITTING STUFF.

STUART YOU ARE MY FAVORITE BUT I HAVE NOTHING TO GIVE YOU EXCEPT I HAVE A SCARF THAT I STARTED KNITTING YOU

I DON'T KNOW IF I'LL FINISH KNITTING IT BEFORE I DIE MAYBE YOUR MOTHER CAN FINISH IT.

SYLVIA THERE IS SOMETHING OUT THERE FOR YOU JUST KEEP LOOKING.

HANNAH YOU ARE SO PRETTY YOU SHOULD GET A NICE HUSBAND OR JUST GET A JOB ONCE AND FOR ALL YOU ARE TOO PRETTY TO BE A WAITRESS.

I KNOW THAT YOU ALL DID NOT ALWAYS LIKE ME ALL I CAN SAY IS THAT I DID MY BEST.

I FELT HATED A LOT BUT ALSO SOMETIMES I FELT LOVED.

HANNAH ALSO I AM SORRY FOR THE THINGS I SAID TO YOU AND EVEN THOUGH IT WAS NOT ACCEPTABLE OR NORMAL FOR YOU TO WRITE LETTERS LIKE THAT OR HAVE A SEXUAL RELATIONSHIP WITH YOUR COUSIN I FORGIVE YOU FOR IT YOU WERE A CHILD AND YOU DID NOT KNOW BETTER.

HANNAH. Could I have that please?

MARNIE. There's more.

LIZZIE. Marnie, knock it off.

HANNAH. Somebody fucking forged that letter.

STUART. *(almost inaudible)* Really?

MARNIE. I WILL NEVER HAVE PEACE KNOWING THAT MY CHILDREN WILL NOT FORGIVE ME AND I AM NOT EVEN SURE WHAT I HAVE DONE THERE IS SOMETHING I CAN SEE IN HERE SORT OF LIKE A PERSON BUT IT IS HARD TO EXPLAIN

AUNT SYLVIA. She's talking about the changeling.

LIZZIE. Marnie, stop it.

MARNIE. I THINK IT MEANS I AM GOING TO DIE SOON. THERE IS ONE LAST THING I NEED TO TELL YOU I AM SORRY ABOUT YOUR FATHER
I BURNED HIS MANUSCRIPT HE WORKED ON IT FOR YEARS BECAUSE OF WHAT HE DID
HE WAS NEVER THE SAME AFTER THAT

And then it's all crossed out. I can't read it.

(to LIZZIE) Can you read it?

LIZZIE. *(not even looking)* No.

MARNIE. And then it says:
I LOVED YOU ALL EVEN SYLVIA.
I DID MY BEST

(stops)

And that's it.

HANNAH. I didn't write that letter.

(pause)

MARNIE. Are you still with Rocco, Hannah? Is he coming by?

AUNT SYLVIA. Daddy never touched me.
And Lizzie wrote that letter.

STUART. *(to LIZZIE)* Is that true?

LIZZIE. Let's not talk about this.

AUNT SYLVIA. The changeling faxed me about that

MARNIE. OK, that's enough. Give me the cup, Sylvia.

AUNT SYLVIA. I want to drink. You're all drinking I want to drink.

MARNIE. You never should have given her alcohol, Lizzie.

(**MARNIE** and **SYLVIA** *tussle over the sippie cup.*)

STUART. Let her have it. Mom, let her have it.
It wasn't a hallucination. The changeling, the whatever it was. I saw it too.

MARNIE. No you did not. Do you understand? You did not see anything.

STUART. Yeah except that I did.

MARNIE. No. You did not.

(*The* **SHAPESHIFTER** *raps at the window.*)

(*The lights go out.*)

(*All see the* **SHAPESHIFTER** *outside.*)

LIZZIE. Oh Jesus what now

(*The lights come back on. The* **SHAPESHIFTER** *is gone.*)

STUART. There.
You see that?

(*pause*)

I said, did you see that?

MARNIE. See what?

STUART. (*to* **HANNAH**) Did you see it?

HANNAH. I don't want to talk about it.

STUART. Lizzie, you saw it.

LIZZIE. Stuart just sit down and drink your drink.

AUNT SYLVIA. She's not going to admit it ever. It's not even worth trying.

STUART. Did you see it? Tell me the truth.

LIZZIE. Sit the fuck down Stuart.

STUART. Can I talk to you for a minute?

LIZZIE. You are talking.

STUART. Alone.

LIZZIE. Why?

STUART. I think you know why.

MARNIE. It feels weird without Ma here. I never thought I'd say that but it does it feels empty somehow, like I can't quite believe it.

LIZZIE. It's always weird like that when an old person dies.

MARNIE. I know, it is, isn't it.

(silence)

(Sound of a fax machine, off.)

LIZZIE. Is your father actually faxing me?

AUNT SYLVIA. It's probably for me.

LIZZIE. Why would someone fax you here?

AUNT SYLVIA. It's the changeling.

MARNIE. Enough, Sylvia.

AUNT SYLVIA. Go check.

(Silence. The fax sound stops.)

Go check.

(Taking her time, **LIZZIE** *exits to go get the fax.)*

(Silence. A pall.)

STUART. So uh. In case anyone was wondering, American Male Comics number fifty-six exceeded expectations. It was towards the bottom of the Diamond charts, number two-ninety-eight, right above an Archie Digest and some Manga thing (that's like Japanese comics) called Sexy Gophers, which, you know, is not great but it gets us some attention from Hollywood, which is what Dipal is uh. Anyway Dipal wanted us to start with number one, so we'd have a greater Uh market presence or whatever, but I really wanted to go with the original numbering, the series ended in 1947, with number fifty-five, unless you count the two issues of American Male's Tales to Shock and Haunt, which I definitely don't, because he just appears as a mailman delivering these like ghoulish letters.

MARNIE. *(to HANNAH)* This is what I always imagined Hell would be like.

STUART. *(hearing but ignoring her)* But we had a few in-store signings and there has been definite interest from retailers. And one of the reviewers, from Comic Satellite dot com, recognized the Chekhov references, which was somewhat satisfying, though he did say it was sort of pretentious. But I've got this whole Borges thing next issue when he gets stuck in a labyrinth and I think in issue three, or fifty-eight actually, I'm going to try and get this whole Thomas Pynchon thing that I haven't quite figured out yet.

(LIZZIE re-enters with the fax.)

LIZZIE. Sylvia, did you give one of your crazy friends our fax number?

AUNT SYLVIA. No. It's from the changeling.

MARNIE. Sylvia will you please stop. Stuart, look at what happens when you go on about your comic books?

STUART. ...What?

HANNAH. What's it say.

LIZZIE. Just a lot of crazy bullshit.

AUNT SYLVIA. You can read it to everybody. It's for me but I don't care. You can read it.

LIZZIE. I'm throwing it out.

HANNAH. Read it. Or I'll read it.

LIZZIE. Who gives a shit. I need to sit down.

(She hands HANNAH the paper and sits. HANNAH reads.)

STUART. What's it say?

AUNT SYLVIA. Go ahead. Read it.

(Beat. HANNAH squints at it.)

HANNAH. ...
   It's hard to read.
   To: Sylvia. From: I can't read what it says here. Something something shake fragrance, gentle bells resound, there stands the something in the something. He something the chalice and he blesses...it...

AUNT SYLVIA. Go ahead.

HANNAH. The handwriting's weird. My…hearts has been a storm…of hate and envy, and it has something, visions of revenge…Oh I have. Dragged virtue from on high, not just with hatred but with. Sinful love.

(stops reading)

I don't know if I.

AUNT SYLVIA. Go ahead. There's nothing bad in there. Nothing we don't all already know.

STUART. How do you know?

MARNIE. Can we stop this? It's just a stupid junk fax, like a spam fax, we get those all the time.

AUNT SYLVIA. Go ahead.

HANNAH. Blood death? Returns with terror at the end, now renewed in power, like a black cloud before the gates of heaven, the last account. I had my husband…murdered?

Aunt Syl, what is this?

I had my husband murdered and something something. O I atoned with every kind of penance but in my soul the worm would not lie still.

AUNT SYLVIA. The worm would not lie still.

MARNIE. Can we stop this now? It's depressing.

STUART. It *is* a funeral.

AUNT SYLVIA. *(re: the fax)* It's almost done.

HANNAH. You imagine your soul can hide from god the sin for which the world condemns you. You will die once on earth for that, confess or stretch your death into the infinite.

Sincerely, I can't make it out.

AUNT SYLVIA. See?

MARNIE. It was like a spam or something. They do them in gibberish now.

STUART. To Aunt Sylvia? And why would someone fax a spam?

MARNIE. It happens all the time.

STUART. Yeah but not that kind of spam, like a gibberish spam, it's always like sales flyers and stuff.

MARNIE. Do you really want to talk about spam on the night of your grandmother's funeral?

STUART. I wasn't.

(not sorry, but placating)

OK, you're right, I'm sorry.

Jesus.

HANNAH. I'm actually.

Actually I'm really sad. I didn't think I would be this sad. Is anyone else sad?

STUART. I'm pretty sad, yeah.

(silence)

HANNAH. I'm going out to sit on the porch.

(pause)

Stuart?

I'm going to sit out on the porch.

STUART. But it's raining.

(realizes)

Oh.

*(She goes out. **STUART** follows her.)*

(The sisters are alone. Ice.)

LIZZIE. That shit's not fucking funny you know.

Those faxes cost money. Dennis has to pay for those.

*(**AUNT SYLVIA** goes into her purse, fishing out change with her hooks.)*

Oh what are you. Stop that.

AUNT SYLVIA. I'll pay for it. I don't want to cost you any money or anything.

LIZZIE. Put your fucking purse away put it away Sylvia.

Sylvia.

Let's just have a drink.

(She pours drinks for them all. They are getting pretty drunk.)

LIZZIE. *(cont.)* Wow. Ma died.

MARNIE. "Ding dong, the witch is dead."

LIZZIE. What the fuck is wrong with you?

MARNIE. What?
I'm sorry. You're right, that was out of line, I'm sorry.

LIZZIE. No forget it.

MARNIE. How is Dennis? Is he still in LA?

LIZZIE. San Diego.

MARNIE. They keep him busy.

LIZZIE. What time is it? He's probably out fucking somebody or something.

(beat)

MARNIE. You seem pretty OK with it.

LIZZIE. What about you?

MARNIE. What about me what?

LIZZIE. Stuart told me you and Ronald were still separated. You gonna make it permanent or what?

MARNIE. I don't know.
We've been talking, he might move into the guest bedroom. I think I told you, he's been living in this terrible neighborhood in Philadelphia, he got jumped by some black kids. All he had was his cell phone and it was so shitty they didn't even take it. They just threw it on the ground.

LIZZIE. Oh my god is he OK?

MARNIE. He's fine. A few bruises and some wounded pride. Not that he has any pride left really.

LIZZIE. Is he…You know?

MARNIE. Is he what?

LIZZIE. Living with someone? In Philly.

(MARNIE laughs. It's genuine.)

Yeah I guess that doesn't sound like him.

MARNIE. I just. I'm pretty terrified, you know. You spend your whole life wanting to be alone and then when you are the first thing you do is wish you weren't alone anymore.

AUNT SYLVIA. Does the changeling visit you?

MARNIE. Sylvia will you knock it off with the goddamn creatures already?

LIZZIE. Marnie.

AUNT SYLVIA. I think it's a legitimate question.

MARNIE. There is no fucking changeling. OK? It was a thing we used to play when we were children, and then we all grew up and we stopped pretending, and because of an extremely tragic and inevitable circumstance, you turned out to have a chemical aberration in your biology that made you unable to separate your reality from our shared childish fantasy. OK?

(silence)

LIZZIE. Why are we even keeping this up anymore?

MARNIE. Keeping what up.

LIZZIE. …Forget it.

AUNT SYLVIA. I go to the church and there's a thing at the church where they talk about love thy enemy. And I was wondering about that, love thy enemy, and thinking what enemy, I don't have an enemy except sometimes the people at the house, sometimes Momo when she goes through my stuff or eats my 'Nilla Wafers which just makes me upset because all she has to do is ask, I like to share with her, but then I thought about the changeling, and everything like that.

(beat; accusatory)

I know you saw it too. Spanish Mary.

MARNIE. Stop, please.

AUNT SYLVIA. You saw it and you lied and told Ma and Daddy that you didn't see anything and that I was seeing things.

MARNIE. It was a child's game Sylvia. Daddy was always filling our heads with nonsense, we made a game out of it.

AUNT SYLVIA. I forgive you.

MARNIE. *(overlapping at the *)* Well, thank you, Sylvia, but there is nothing for you to forgive me for, I have taken care of you, I have looked after *you –

LIZZIE. *(overlapping at the *)* *Will you knock it off, Marnie?

MARNIE. Knock what off?

LIZZIE. She's telling the truth, we saw the fucking thing, we lied, I'm sorry Sylvia, I'm sorry, I'm sorry we ruined your life, we were kids, what's done is done, Jesus we ruined your fucking life.

(She cries a little.)

MARNIE. Maybe we should stop drinking.

AUNT SYLVIA. I forgive you Lizzie.

MARNIE. You're being maudlin.

LIZZIE. Do you realize what we did to her? The, I don't even want to go into it now, the fucking shock treatments, the goddamn, the drugs, she got raped by an orderly!

MARNIE. You don't need to bring that up.

AUNT SYLVIA. I forgave that boy too.

MARNIE. *(overlapping at the *)* Ma should have paid for her to go to a decent institution. OK? I am sorry that she just threw her in that state home shithole, and Sylvia, it breaks my heart every time I think of it, but you and I can not bear *responsibility for –

LIZZIE. *(overlapping at the *)* *WE SAW IT! OK? We saw the fucking whatever it was, we talked about seeing it, we talked about what we were going to say when they decided to send her away.

MARNIE. We were children. And you know, did it ever occur to you that you were also hallucinating?

LIZZIE. Then what was it you were seeing?

MARNIE. These, these boogeymen aren't real, Lizzie, we're grown women, it's about time we *stopped –

(The lights go out at the *.)

LIZZIE. Oh what the fuck now.

AUNT SYLVIA. You shouldn't talk about it like that.

LIZZIE. I wasn't talking about the thing I was talking about the lights.

AUNT SYLVIA. I meant Marnie.

MARNIE. It's probably just like a blown fuse or something. Is it all the power or just the light?

(Sound of LIZZIE flicking things on and off.)

LIZZIE. I think it's everything.

MARNIE. Do you have a flashlight?

(sound of rustling through cabinet)

LIZZIE. Fuck.

MARNIE. What?

LIZZIE. Dennis has all that shit out in the garage, I don't know where he keeps any of it.

(sound of a fax in the other room)

MARNIE. There's power in the office.

LIZZIE. The light's off in there too.

AUNT SYLVIA. Spanish Mary doesn't need electricity to fax her messages.

(Pause as the fax comes through. It's long.)

(It stops.)

MARNIE. You going to go get it?

LIZZIE. It's dark.

MARNIE. I'll go get it.

LIZZIE. We can't read it in the dark anyway.
Sit down, let's just drink.

(Silence for a little while.)

Anyway Sylvia I'm sorry we ruined your life.

AUNT SYLVIA. It's OK. You didn't ruin my life. I'm still alive. I'm happier than you. I'm happier than Marnie.

MARNIE. She's got a point.

LIZZIE. Do you still have sex?
MARNIE. Not really.
LIZZIE. I meant Sylvia.
MARNIE. Don't be gross.
LIZZIE. For real. I think about that.
AUNT SYLVIA. I met a man who likes my stumps.
LIZZIE. *(overlapping)* What?!
MARNIE. *(overlapping)* Ew!
AUNT SYLVIA. It's not like that, he's nice. Anyway I had my share of that stuff in my time. He just likes to look at them and touch them a little and he does his thing and then we cuddle for a while.

(They laugh with a sort of girlish, grossed-out glee.)

MARNIE. Sylvia, honey, I'm sorry but that is creepy.
AUNT SYLVIA. He's not creepy he's nice. He makes a lot of money, you know. He's very successful. He's a lawyer.
LIZZIE. How did you meet him?
AUNT SYLVIA. At the library I go on the world wide web and they have bulletin boards for this.
LIZZIE. Is he hot?
MARNIE. Lizzie!
AUNT SYLVIA. He's a very dignified and attractive older man. I think, no actually I know he's married and has two daughters in college.
MARNIE. Well at least we know it's not Dennis.
LIZZIE. Or Ronald.
MARNIE. It might be Ronald, he's proposed worse.
   I'm sorry, Sylvia, I didn't mean.
AUNT SYLVIA. It's OK I know it's weird. At least I'm not lonely.

(silence)

MARNIE. This is OK, you know? This is kind of nice. Talking to you. I think this family is always at our best when we're grieving.

(The lights come back on.)

LIZZIE. Fucking fuses.

MARNIE. You should call a guy to come fix it. A hot young guy in a tank top with a what do you call it, a mullet hairdo.

LIZZIE. Ugh, no.

MARNIE. What, you don't like that? Like Billy Ray Cyrus.

LIZZIE. You're fucking foul.

(They drink.)

MARNIE. You want me to go see what that fax was?

AUNT SYLVIA. What's the hurry?

(beat)

LIZZIE. There's something I feel like I should tell you. It's weird.

*(Abruptly, **HANNAH** comes in, damp from the rain. All look at her.)*

HANNAH. What?

MARNIE. How's everything going out there? Still raining?

HANNAH. I'm just coming in to get some beers for me and Stuart.

(She gets the beer. No one speaks. She goes to exit, stops:)

We're talking. About a lot of things, Mom. I think he's going to want to talk to you.

LIZZIE. What do you mean.

(She walks out, slamming the door behind her.)

(beat)

MARNIE. What were you going to tell us?

LIZZIE. Nothing.

MARNIE. OK.

(They drink.)

Is it about Ronald?

LIZZIE. Is what about Ronald?

MARNIE. The thing you were going to tell me but then you changed your mind.

LIZZIE. No.

MARNIE. He used to have the hots for you.

LIZZIE. What? Ugh.

No offense.

MARNIE. I feel much the same way.

He would tell me about these fantasies. That he would have about you.

LIZZIE. I really don't want to hear about it.

MARNIE. What were you going to tell me?

LIZZIE. Nothing. Seriously, it's nothing.

(Silence. They drink.)

AUNT SYLVIA. I'm going to get that fax.

LIZZIE. Knock yourself out.

(She exits.)

(long pause)

MARNIE. You can tell me if it's about Ronald.

LIZZIE. I am not attracted to fucking Ronald. OK? I was never attracted to Ronald. Not even when we were young, he had B.O. and that horrible fucking moustache. He looked like a child molester.

MARNIE. What is it you wanted to tell me then?

LIZZIE. I don't know Marnie it was nothing.

(beat)

We should have told Ma about Spanish Mary.

MARNIE. It was a game will you please shut up about Spanish Mary.

LIZZIE. It was not a game.

MARNIE. I'm not talking about this with you.

LIZZIE. We fucking destroyed her Marnie, just look at her.

MARNIE. She's happier than we are.

(beat)

LIZZIE. Where is she. Sylvia, you OK in there?

(No answer. They drink.)

(LIZZIE mutters something that sounds a little like, "I fucked your son. A lot.")

MARNIE. What? Don't mumble.

LIZZIE. Nothing.

(STUART and HANNAH re-enter, wet from rain.)

HANNAH. Please stop crying Stuart.

STUART. I'm not, I'm sorry just.

(He goes to the cognac and pours himself some more.)

HANNAH. I don't think you should drink any more.

STUART. Yeah, well.

(He chugs some cognac, runs to the sink, and pukes. He spits a little, maybe rinses his mouth out, maybe not, and drinks some more. All wince.)

MARNIE. So how's the backyard?

HANNAH. *(looking at LIZZIE)* I'm actually genuinely speechless.

LIZZIE. What.

HANNAH. Really, Mom? I mean, really?

MARNIE. What is everyone on about?

HANNAH. I feel like I should call the police.

STUART. Don't.

(AUNT SYLVIA re-enters, holding the fax in her hooks.)

LIZZIE. Anything interesting?

AUNT SYLVIA. I always knew this day would happen. When Ma and Daddy came up the stairs, they had the man with the necktie waiting out front, and I wanted to sing the car song but no one would.
My first night in that place, the little bed was hard and they didn't give me enough blankets, and Spanish Mary's head appeared on my wall like a filmstrip, and she said one day, one day. That's all she said, but I

knew what she meant. For a long time it would look like you had everything and I had nothing but one day something would happen and I would be happier than both of you put together, and on that day I could forgive you.

AUNT SYLVIA. *(cont.)* And I do forgive you.

Except I'm not really that happy, not really.

(re. the fax)

Remember Daddy would come home from the bus and sit in the little side room listening to classical music and he would look at the German until it was like he was blind? Remember?

(She waits for an answer from her sisters. Nothing.)

How about the fire? Remember that?

(still nothing)

One night after they sent me away, I wasn't here for this, the changeling told me about it, Daddy came home from the bus and everything he worked on was in a big black pile of ashes and soot in the kitchen sink. The walls were black and the curtains were black and everything smelled like smoke for weeks after that.

Did I get that part right, Marnie?

(no answer)

He loved that one German play, it was by Schiller, from Stuart's statue.

(beat)

After Ma burned it he never translated anything ever again.

But the thing is, nothing ever goes away, not really. I have Daddy's translation right here.

It says on the fax cover sheet it's for Stuart.

Do you want to hear it?

STUART. No thank you, Sylvia.

AUNT SYLVIA. I think you should hear it.

(she reads)
Am I alive? How can my body live?
How can the ceiling stretch above my head,
Not crashing on me? Why does no abyss
Open to swallow this reproach to nature!
Ah faithless man! It is for you no longer
To turn to tender rain. The road you follow
Leads far from love. Defend your mind with mortar,
With a smooth face, unscaleable as ice.
You must hold fast to evil to the end –
Or see the prize of your misdeed pass by.
Compassion, turn your gaze upon a gorgon
Within, and be a stone.

STUART. Aunt Sylvia, please stop it.

AUNT SYLVIA. I cannot. I cannot! Cannot move towards that horror. Oh, they are moving under me already, downstairs, the deed is being set in motion. They speak.

(He goes to tear the fax from her hooks. It's pretty well in there. They struggle for a bit throughout the following:)

(Until both of them fall into the table of food, and then to the ground, making a mess of things.)

LIZZIE. Jesus, what the fuck –

STUART. I told you to STOP Sylvia –

(In the food, **AUNT SYLVIA** *moves to kiss him.)*

STUART. Ugh, stop it, what are you STOP.

LIZZIE. Jesus Christ, will you look at this, what is wrong with you two –

*(***STUART*** takes a big handful of casserole or something and wings it at* **LIZZIE.***)*

STUART that's my good black dress what the fuck is wrong with you.

STUART. Who wrote that letter.

LIZZIE. What letter.

STUART. The pink one.

LIZZIE. I don't know what you're talking about.

STUART. *(to* **HANNAH***)* You want to tell her what you told me?

HANNAH. I'm skeeved, you two work this out amongst yourselves.

STUART. Hey Mom, you want to know who I lost my virginity with?

LIZZIE. Stuart, stop it.

AUNT SYLVIA. *(in the food)* Will somebody help me up please?

MARNIE. Stuart help your Aunt up.

STUART. How I can't even get up myself.

MARNIE. Well this is some funeral huh.

(**STUART** *throws some food at* **MARNIE.**)

Stuart!

(**LIZZIE** *throws food at* **MARNIE** *too.*)

(*They have a small food fight. They all get caught in the crossfire.*)

(*It ends. Beat.*)

STUART. OK. You want to know what's really going on, everybody?

You probably don't but who gives a shit.

I got this letter, shoved into the pocket of my coat on Thanksgiving. It said a lot of things, but at the end it told me to wait in this one parking lot. I waited and Hannah never showed but I saw Aunt Lizzie's car with Aunt Lizzie in it.

I was upset, I cried, and Lizzie gave me a hug and one thing led to another I guess and it kept happening, all through eighth grade and most of high school, even in college a few times.

That was why I never had a girlfriend, Mom. OK? In case you were wondering, which I imagine you were, because you were always asking about it.

MARNIE. ... Is this true?

LIZZIE. No.

HANNAH. What the fuck, Mom.

LIZZIE. It's not true. He's sick. Just like the whole Spanish Mary thing isn't true.

STUART. What the fuck, Lizzie.

MARNIE. I think you need help, Stuart.

HANNAH. Aunt Marnie, come on.

MARNIE. What, Hannah? You're telling me you believe this? You need help, Stuart. I always thought you needed help.

STUART. What, are you going to have me committed like you did to Sylvia?

MARNIE. I didn't do that.
Anyway you're an adult, I can't have you committed unless you're planning on doing something dangerous. Are you planning on doing something dangerous?

STUART. What? Like what?

MARNIE. He's obsessive, Hannah. I hate to say this about my own son, but you might want to consider getting a restraining order.

STUART. A what? Come the fuck on, Mom, tell her Lizzie.

LIZZIE. We never did anything. I'm sorry, Stuart, but this whole fantasy thing is really fucked up.

HANNAH. Who wrote that letter then?

MARNIE. Isn't it obvious? He wrote it himself.

(beat)

HANNAH. Did you?

STUART. Of course not!

MARNIE. Delusional behavior runs in our family.

STUART. What the fuck! Mom!

(sound of the fax, off)

(beat)

AUNT SYLVIA. She's really talkative tonight.

(Beat. The fax stops.)

I'll get it.

(She works her way up, gruelingly, perhaps sliding in the food. No one helps her. She goes.)

MARNIE. Honey I'm sorry but I think this all happened in your head.

STUART. Fuck that. It happened. Lizzie tell them.

LIZZIE. Stuart this is just weird.

STUART. *(to* **HANNAH**) You believe me, don't you?

HANNAH. I honestly don't know who to believe anymore.

I'm going to go. Like for real.

I don't think I'm going to come back for a while.

AUNT SYLVIA. *(re-entering)* Just wait a minute.

HANNAH. Why Sylvia.

AUNT SYLVIA. The changeling has something it would like to tell you all.

HANNAH. I don't know if I want to hear it.

AUNT SYLVIA. No one ever wants to hear it.

(The doorbell rings. It's an elaborate chime.)

That's my cue.

We can't be in the same room together.

(She exits out back.)

(The bell rings again.)

STUART. Is someone going to get that?

(It rings again.)

(And again.)

OK, fine.

(He works his way up out of the food mess and goes to the door, but the zombified **SHAPESHIFTER** *is already there, in the form of* **RUTHIE**. *Beat.)*

(No one is exactly surprised to see her but they're not happy she's there.)

SHAPESHIFTER/RUTHIE. Hep hep hep hep!
   I am going to designate this for you:
   This one in whose cast I reside is boggled here, trussed in scotch with me, because she was the sticky one who actuated me here, who first bindled the myriad abounding genitalia of her unspoken self into mounds in the corners like so many cocks of dust. It was she who headmost pined to snuff the loud hairy breathing of her benedict, your Vater and Großvater, and did she? That secret evanesces. But we know it was she who nursed the murderous heart which now resides in the bosoms of you sticky ones.
   You have a choice: you can confess it all and I will adjourn like a breeze. Or you can bump as you have ever bumped and I shall abide, in the cast of this one and this one in the cast of me, like handwriting thrust upward through the fresh dirt, ever abeyant, just outside of your hedgerows and inside your fax machines, texting you at times that will always be inconvenient, hiding under your beds, wrapped in my shroud of yarn and quilts, you will smell my funk before you hear my sonance and hear my sonance before you see me and you will always see me oh yes oh yes that will most ineluctably will bump.
   OK that's enough of that.
   I will leave you to it then. I am going to annex this soda pop if no one boggles.
   Poof.

   (She takes a bottle of soda and goes.)

STUART. Well?

MARNIE. Shut up, Stuart.

STUART. I'm not going to fucking shut up. You heard her.

MARNIE. I didn't hear anything.

STUART. Are you fucking kidding me? You heard her. If we don't admit all of this she'll haunt us forever.

MARNIE. Admit all of what.

STUART. Jesus. Lizzie, Hannah, help me out here.

HANNAH. I think I'm gonna go.

STUART. Come on.

HANNAH. If I go now I can still catch the last connecting train in Secaucus.

STUART. Let me give you a ride at least.

HANNAH. I'd rather walk.

STUART. Please don't go.

HANNAH. Uh
   Sorry but.
   'Bye.

   (She goes.)

STUART. Please.

   *(**AUNT SYLVIA** enters from the back porch.)*

AUNT SYLVIA. Well?
   Did she tell you all?

LIZZIE. No one was at the door.

STUART. Aunt Lizzie, come on.

LIZZIE. Just kids. They ring and run, you know.
   Let's get this shit cleaned up.

STUART. You saw it, it was right here. We have to talk about this stuff.

LIZZIE. It's been a long night let's at least get some of this stuff cleaned so it doesn't get all crusty for tomorrow.

STUART. Lizzie please.

AUNT SYLVIA. You shouldn't expect any different, Stuart. I told you.

STUART. Please.

   *(Silence. **LIZZIE** starts to clean.)*

   Please.

MARNIE. Honey. You'll thank us for this later.

   *(She joins **LIZZIE** in cleaning. Beat.)*

   *(**STUART** freaks out. He starts tossing all of the food everywhere. He is truly fearsome – they all get out of the way.)*

(He makes a real mess of things. He stands in the center of his mess, hyperventilating.)

(From somewhere in the mess, the "Doctor Who" theme plays. It's tinny. It plays a couple of times, like it's on a loop. **STUART** *digs through his pockets, and through the food, eventually coming up with a cell phone.)*

(He opens it, the music stops. He checks the caller ID, answers.)

STUART. Hey Dipal, what's up.
Nothing much, really, you know my grandma.
Yeah thanks.
OK.
OK.
Great, that's great.
Sure, I can. Sure, Tuesday's good.
OK, great.
No, congratulations to you, too.
OK, yeah, thanks.
Talk to you soon.
Yeah.
(He hangs up. Beat.)
Good news.
Dipal sold the film rights to American Male.
I think I'm a millionaire. They have to work out all the paperwork and a lot of that is back end so I won't see it for a while but.

(beat)

MARNIE. That's great. That's great honey. Now what do you say we get this cleaned up.

(beat)

STUART. OK.

(They do not clean but stand, silent, in the mess.)

(The **SHAPESHIFTER** *looks in through the back window.)*

(Lights fade.)

End of Play

PROPERTIES

Set:

Kitchen # 1 Bucks County PA McMansion
  Unopened mail
  Fridge
  Stove
  Cabinets
  Island with sink
  2 stools

Kitchen #2 Bergen County NJ Retro Kitchen
  Fridge
  Stove
  Sink
  Cabinets
  Wastebasket
  Window

Center:
  Kitchen table
  6 chairs
  Outside deck with 2 lawn chairs
  Wind chimes

Hand Props:
Act 1
  Sketch pad
  Box with bust of Schiller
  Box with Flintstone glasses
  Box of childhood items
  Newspapers
  Pink letter (repeated in many scenes)
  Powder
  Soda #1
  Stewart's cell phone
  Cabinet dressing: pots, pans, plates, etc
  Cutting board
  Vegetables
  Walker
  Olives in jar
  Grapes
  News magazine
  Broken bust of Schiller (repeated)

Gorilla Glue
Cleaning supplies
Soda #2
Placemats
Hannah's cell phone
Food for preparation
Carrot sticks
Aunt Ruthie's purse
Shopping bag
Kalamata olives
Repaired Bust of Schiller (repeated)
Wine bottle
Corkscrew
Large container of cheese balls
Stubbed out cigarette
Aunt Sylvia's purse
Diet Sprite
Powder
Soda #3 (Diet Sprite)
Hors'dourves
Small dish
Birthday cake
Candles for cake
Icing
Dirty dishes

Act 2
Portfolio
Easel
Bust of Schiller
Drawing pencils
Clip light
Bulk size Teddy Grahams
Fax #1
Coffee maker
Coffee
Keys
Bowl
lighter
Smoke Detector
Soda #4 (Ginger Ale)
Spread of food
Bottle of Cognac
4 glasses

Sippie cup
The Will
Fax #2
Well worn fax
Aunt Sylvia's purse
Pocket change
6 pack of beer
Fax #3
Puke
Casserole Dish
Soda #4
Stuart's Cell Phone (repeated)

OTHER TITLES AVAILABLE FROM SAMUEL FRENCH

1001

Jason Grote

4m, 2f to play multiple roles / Dramatic Comedy

The cuckolded King Shahriyar is marrying a new bride every night and beheading her the next morning. As unrest spreads in the Sultanate, his vizier's daughter Scheherazade hatches a plan: she will offer herself as a bride and seduce the king with stories that leave him hanging on every word. She weaves such tales as "Sinbad the Sailor" and "Aladdin and His Magic Lamp" with stories of Borges, Flaubert, and Alan and Dahna – a Jewish man and an Arab woman who have fallen in love in millennial New York City. Shahriyar becomes Alan and Scheherazade becomes Dahna as the worlds mingle and inform one another. Modern speech invades the fantasy tales, and swords and genii appear in the 21st Century, in a dance of cultures and people who are forever intertwined.

"[An] explosive, often brilliant work about America, narrative, the Middle East and identity."
– *Time Out New York*

"...funny, moving, postmodernist-in-a-good-way... Like Scheherazade's tales, *1001* is endlessly compelling, and also endless (again, in a good way)..."
– *Boston Globe*

"Jason Grote is one of a generation of brainy new American dramatists – including Tracy Letts and Will Eno – who understand that to reach new audiences, political theater needs to move beyond moral indignation and outrage, past spoon-feeding an attitude. One key to going forward is looking backward into literature, fable and allegory."
– *LA Weekly*

SAMUELFRENCH.COM

OTHER TITLES AVAILABLE FROM SAMUEL FRENCH

FEVER/DREAM

Sheila Callaghan

Comedy / 3m, 3f, flexible casting

Chained to his desk in the basement of customer service hell, Segis suddenly finds himself set free in the CEO's penthouse—but is it a dream? This raucous reinvention of Pedro Calderón de la Barca's *Life is a Dream* gleefully skewers corporate America with razor-sharp wit

"Enjoyably stylish [with an] antic pace and witty aesthetic"
– *Washington Post*

"Ambitious, often uproarious."
– *City Paper*

"A pizzazz-filled concoction that skewers corporatism with a generous supply side of laughs. [Callaghan] is without doubt the purveyor of top-shelf American wit."
– *Metro Weekly*

"[Callaghan has] a keen eye for the outlandish. Exudes the kind of infectious zaniness that occasionally attracts cult followings."
– *Variety*

"I can't remember the last time a play made me laugh so hard. Between the chuckles and belly laughs, the dialog is surprisingly layered, and gives the audience plenty to think about. *Fever/Dream* is about as funny as the sharpest Hollywood comedy, and far more rewarding."
–*BrightestYoungThings.com*

SAMUELFRENCH.COM